# STAR TREK®
## Celebrations

# STAR TREK®
## Celebrations

## MAUREEN McTIGUE

**POCKET BOOKS**

NEW YORK  LONDON  TORONTO  SYDNEY  SINGAPORE

An *Original* Publication of POCKET BOOKS

POCKET BOOKS, a division of Simon & Schuster, Inc.
1230 Avenue of the Americas, New York, NY 10020

ISBN: 0-7434-1773-9

First Pocket Books trade paperback printing September 2001

10 9 8 7 6 5 4 3 2 1

POCKET and colophon are registered trademarks of
Simon & Schuster, Inc.

For information regarding special discounts for bulk purchases,
please contact Simon & Schuster Special Sales at 1-800-456-6798 or
business@simonandschuster.com

Designed by Joseph Rutt

Printed in the U.S.A.

# INTRODUCTION

As in "Data's Day," Data points out, "Besides the arrival of Ambassador T'Pel, other events occurring today include four birthdays, two personnel transfers, a celebration of the Hindu Festival of Lights, two chess tournaments, one secondary school play, and four promotions.

"Overall . . . an ordinary day."

About Klingons in particular, during the events in "Looking for *par'Mach* in All the Wrong Places," Quark notes, "Come on! There has to be another way out of this! You people have rituals for everything except waste extraction . . . you must have a ceremony or a secret handshake or *something* I can do."

Saying that Starfleet and the life-forms it interacts with don't have a fair share of rituals and celebrations is to miss a fantastical side of it all. Any culture can be experienced through its celebrations, from weddings to funerals to rites of passage. The Klingons and Bajorans seem to have a ritual for almost everything they do, but that reflects who they are. Bajorans are spiritual, Klingons are warriors, but their every move stands for something.

This book is an attempt to encapsulate the celebrations that have permeated *Star Trek* throughout the years. So enjoy the fun—and remember, there is no Klingon word for joy!

—*Maureen McTigue*

# ONE

*Federation*

*and*

*Starfleet*

# FIRST CONTACT DAY

In the years and months leading up to April 7, 2063, Zefram Cochrane tested a transport system that would change Earth.

In 2063, he perfected a warp drive, making possible faster-than-light travel. His test of this system caught the attention of a Vulcan ship traveling past Earth. The Vulcans investigated, meeting Cochrane and initiating interplanet relations. With Earth's newfound flight capabilities, humans were able to move past their warlike nature and join together, eventually leading to the United Federation of Planets.

April 7 is the most celebrated day in Federation history. It is the one day that unites all the life-forms that fall under the flag. The traditional Vulcan greeting of "Live long and prosper," along with the split-fingered salute, is used by all on this day.

On Earth, the Montana area on the North American continent is the location of the largest festivities. Earth families gather to celebrate the peace and prosperity that Cochrane led their planet to; interstellar peoples join in celebrating the unity of their planets. This is an official holiday for all cadets at the Academy and offices of the Federation and Starfleet in all sectors.

Fireworks, which were used to celebrate many joyous occasions in ancient Earth cultures, are used here, but are enhanced by flight performances of Starfleet pilots and cadets. The *Phoenix* comes out of the Smithsonian and is put on public display. This is the day, annually, when the Cochrane Medal of Excellence is awarded.

It is this day when the new future began, when warp engines were the norm, when the Federation was born and people across the galaxy began to boldly go where no one has gone before.

# FEDERATION DAY

Much like First Contact Day, Federation Day is a cross-cultural celebration. The forming of the United Federation of Planets in 2161, one hundred years after First Contact, was the continuation of what Zefram Cochrane and the Vulcans achieved the previous century.

The celebration of Federation Day is not as elaborate as that of First Contact Day. Federation offices work with a reduced staff, allowing for members to reflect on the day. Each of the one hundred and fifty planets in the Federation has its own way of celebrating this particular day, though many will also celebrate their particular admittance day. Parades and pageants are held in the Earth cities San Francisco and Paris, where the Federation Council and the Federation President meet and reside respectively.

# STARFLEET

With the joining of cross-cultural intergalactic lives, Starfleet is the operating scientific, exploratory, and defensive agency for the United Federation of Planets. The Prime Directive is one of the primary tenets of Starfleet. The Prime Directive states that Starfleet personnel and spacecraft may not interfere in the normal development of any society, and mandates that any vessel or crew member is expendable to prevent violation of this rule.

The intricacies of Starfleet life begin within the prestigious halls of Starfleet Academy, found in San Francisco, Earth, not far from the main Command Center.

## Life of a Cadet

The four years of Starfleet Academy can be the hardest but most rewarding of a person's life. Getting into the Academy means that you have proven yourself to be among the best and the brightest in the Federation. If you aren't a member of the Federation, and you have proven your merit to a ranking member of Starfleet, they may sponsor your admittance. That, in and of itself, is admirable, as proven by Nog, the first Ferengi ever admitted into the Academy. Captain Benjamin Sisko was his sponsor; as fate would have it, serving under Sisko at that time was Lieutenant Commander Worf, the first Klingon to serve in Starfleet.

A combination of academic study, physical attributes, and ship's duty, as well as extracurricular activities, leads to a well-rounded Academy education. The first thing a cadet will learn is the Academy's motto:

*Ex astris, scientia.*

This ancient Earth Latin means:

From the stars, knowledge.

Cadets are first put through an orientation program to get them used to a regimented lifestyle. Over the course of the four years, basic training gives way to advanced study, which enhances each factor of their lives.

An honor code is inherent in the training. Honor, personal integrity, and loyalty to the service, its customs, and its traditions are fundamental characteristics essential to a successful officer. Loyalty to fellow cadets is also held in high regard.

Over the years, a cadet may find that his or her strength lies in a specific field, and may choose one of many course specifics after completing all the required courses of a plebe (or first-year student). Course offerings in engineering, medicine, security, command, flight, space exploration, tactical situations, survival, and protocol are available. Cadets are encouraged to join one of the many organizations that give them time to utilize what they've learned, whether it be with a sports organization, with medical personnel, or within a flight squadron. One third-year course includes a six-week focus on space walks so that extravehicular activity becomes familiar.

There have been times when cadets have been negligent in observing strict protocol related to piloting procedures. Abuse of this kind can lead to injury or death and should be treated with the utmost gravity. Cadets found derelict in their observance of such protocol are dealt with in harsh disciplinary actions, which may result in expulsion from the Academy.

A few of the extracurricular teams the cadets can join, if they demonstrate sufficient prowess, include some squadrons that have entertained and astonished their classmates over the years. Nova Squadron is an elite group of five cadets who are some of the best single-pilot flyers at the Academy. Members of another elite group, Red Squad, are specially chosen for highly specialized training. Only cadets who have proven themselves in academic and field endeavors are even considered for the squad. Commemorating the sacrifice of Red Squad during the Dominion War, two special service awards—the *Valiant* commendation for teamwork, and the Watters Ribbon of Valor for leadership—have been established for cadets.

After the work of four years, including flight time and actual field service on a ship, graduation is the most joyous occasion of a cadet's academic life. The large affair has all the pomp and circumstance accorded those who reach this pinnacle of study. Cadets are granted their ensign commissions, and a display of flight prowess is performed by some of the highest-ranking members of the graduating class as they all prepare to step into the leadership roles they will hold in the years to come. A graduate of command rank is asked to give the commencement speech to honor the work that has been done by members of the graduating class, and to welcome the cadets into active service.

History has shown, though, that a cadet's Academy time may not represent the officer he will become. Two well-respected *Enterprise* captains provide noteworthy examples of this. James T. Kirk was a noted bookworm at the Academy and was observed to be "on the dull side," but he would come to be known as one of Starfleet's boldest commanders. Captain Jean-Luc Picard almost didn't graduate from the Academy. He got into fights on a regular basis, and failed in his first attempt to be admitted to the Academy. He did eventually receive full academic honors and is now one of Starfleet's most highly regarded captains.

Starfleet Academy has a way of finding a cadet's strength and succeeding in making it stronger.

# Officer Promotion

## Traditional Promotion

Benjamin L. Sisko from commander to captain (Stardate 48959.1).

Presiding over the promotion ceremony, as is the custom, Jake Sisko, son of Benjamin Sisko, pins the new pip on his father's collar.

Jake looks solemn as he says, "Dad, there's something I've been wanting to say to you for a long time. And now that I finally have the chance, I'm going to make it short and simple. Congratulations, Captain."

"Though I don't fully understand this humanoid obsession with rank and title," notes Security Chief Odo, "if anyone deserves to be promoted, it's you."

Chief Miles O'Brien offers the toast: "To the newest, and best, captain in Starfleet. All I can say is it's about time."

## Merit Promotion

Counselor Deanna Troi from lieutenant commander to commander (Stardate 47611).

Passing the bridge officer exam to achieve command status isn't as easy as it sounds. Deanna Troi failed her tests at first because she refused to allow any of her simulated crew to die. Though she eventually earned the promotion, Troi wasn't convinced that she deserved it. Commander Riker explained, "You tried every alternative, looked at all the options, and in the end you made the hard choice."

Ezri Dax from ensign to lieutenant junior grade and counselor.

Deciding to live on Space Station Deep Space 9 as the Dax symbiont had in its previous host, Jadzia, Ezri Dax is promoted into a position that will allow her to better serve the station. Starfleet Medical waived the rest of her counselor training and gave her the commission as full counselor with rank of lieutenant (j.g.) on the recommendation of Captain Sisko. His theory was that there wasn't much they could teach Ezri in a few months that the Dax symbiont hadn't learned in the last three hundred years.

## Private Celebrations

On a nineteenth-century battleship christened *Enterprise,* Lieutenant Worf is granted promotion to lieutenant commander in a private ceremony conducted by his fellow officers, Captain Picard, Commander Riker, Commander Beverly Crusher, M.D., Lieutenant Commander Data, and Lieutenant Commander Geordi La Forge. Their uniforms reflect the ancient times that the ship hails from.

Riker reads from a piece of parchment:

"We, the officers and crew of the *U.S.S. Enterprise,* being of sound mind and judgment, hereby make the

following charges against Lieutenant Worf. One, that he did knowingly and willfully perform above and beyond the call of duty on countless occasions. Two, most seriously that he has earned the admiration and respect of the entire crew."

Picard concludes the ceremony:

"Mr. Worf, I hereby promote you to the rank of lieutenant commander with all the rights and privileges thereto. And may God have mercy on your soul."

The assembled crew congratulates the Klingon. But their ceremony is not over.

Worf then has to walk the plank and try to reach the badge of office, an officer's hat, which is hanging directly above the plank. Worf jumps, grabs the hat off the rope, and lands back on the plank without losing his balance and falling into the ocean . . . which, according to Riker, has never been done.

"If there's one thing I've learned over the years," Picard says, "it's never underestimate a Klingon."

## Field Promotion

On occasion, a cadet is given a promotion to ensign, signifying his contributions. There are different situations for field promotions. On the *Starship Enterprise*, Wesley Crusher, who had not yet begun Academy work, had assisted the engineering crew after failed warp-drive experiments. On Stardate 41263.4, he was granted all duties and privileges of the rank of acting ensign. He was expected to apply to Starfleet Academy at the first opportunity.

Although not yet at the Academy, Crusher received another field promotion, this time to ensign, after assisting on a rescue mission. He then went on to the Academy for official training.

Nog , the first Ferengi ever to attend Starfleet Academy, was back on Deep Space 9 for a field study assignment when the station fell under attack by Dominion forces. His field promotion was a battlefield commission to ensign (2374). At the conclusion of the war, Nog was promoted to lieutenant, one of Captain Sisko's final acts before he joined the Bajoran Prophets.

# Death Rituals

Starfleet and the Federation recognize and acknowledge the individual beliefs of each and every one of their members, from the youngest cadet to the oldest admiral. Some ancient Earth traditions, for examples, have been an integral part of Starfleet since its origins. These traditions mean a great deal to humans, since death rituals tend to honor a comrade who has fallen in the line of duty. It has been noted by some life-forms uninitiated in the ways of humanoids that "human attitudes toward death are perplexing." As the former Borg, Seven of Nine, on the *Starship Voyager* notes:

> "Too much importance is placed on it. There seem to be countless rituals and cultural beliefs designed to alleviate their fear of a simple biological truth: all organisms eventually perish."

But, as Captain Kirk once told the Vulcan Lieutenant Saavik:

> "How we deal with death is at least as important as how we deal with life."

In ancient times, on wooden ships, the crew would commend the deceased to the sea—a burial at sea—so that the sea, having taken the life, would get the body in return. As ships advanced and moved into the stars, the tradition of launching the body into the void of space—burial in a sea of stars—began and continues to this day.

When Captain Spock, one of the most highly regarded members of Starfleet, died saving the *Enterprise* after it had been sabotaged by Khan Noonien Singh, he was given the traditional Starfleet burial accorded the honored dead (Stardate 8130.3).

The crew was on deck, at relaxed attention, watching a tor-

pedo tube casing that had been converted to a casket, draped in the Federation flag, pass. The captain, Kirk, said:

> "We are assembled here today to pay final respects to our honored dead. And yet it should be noted that in the midst of our sorrow, this death takes place in the shadow of new life, the sunrise of a new world, a world that our beloved comrade gave his life to protect and nourish. He did not feel this sacrifice a vain or empty one, and we will not debate his profound wisdom at these proceedings. Of my friend, I can only say this: Of all the souls I have encountered, his was the most . . . human."

The crew was called to strict attention, as Commander Montgomery Scott played "Amazing Grace" on the bagpipes, and the torpedo is blasted into space, concluding an intergalactic burial in the cosmos.

When faced with honoring their dead, a crew will attempt to find a middle ground that honors the beliefs of the fallen, while incorporating them into a Starfleet service. It is frequently the human custom to conduct a solemn, dignified service in which the dead are praised by their friends and loved ones. The basics of any funerary custom are to say a ritual farewell. But that farewell need not be solemn. On the *U.S.S. Enterprise* (NCC 1701-D), a ship that had seen her fair share of death as well as success, the apparent loss of Commander Geordi La Forge and Ensign Ro Laren provoked a different memorial (2368, Stardate 45892.4). This wake was a festive occasion, with crew members sharing happy memories of the fallen. Ten-Forward was full of

people in full party mode, there was a lively atmosphere, the place was brightly lit, there was food and drink, and a jazz combo played an upbeat tune. La Forge would later comment to his comrades that he thought the memorial service was perfect.

The crew of the *U.S.S. Defiant* (NX-74205), on a recon mission (Stardate 51948.3), discovers Captain Lisa Cusak, a long-dead Starfleet officer. Subspace transmissions allow them to speak to her. But the officer had died long before the crew of the *Defiant* ever departed from Deep Space 9. Following their devastating discovery, the crew decides to recover her remains and hold a service on DS9.

The wardroom on DS9 was the setting for an Irish wake. Music, food, and drink are plenty. The mood is celebratory. At one end of the room, in front of the large monitor, lies a photon torpedo casing that, once again, serves as a casket. The torpedo has a Federation flag draped over it and is surrounded by flowers.

By tradition, an Irish wake is a boisterous affair. There is singing, laughing, and drinking, and stories are told of the deceased. It's a time to memorialize the dead and celebrate life at the same time. In a way, it bears a resemblance to Klingon death rituals.

During *Voyager*'s time in the Delta Quadrant, Captain Kathryn Janeway died—apparently—in a shuttle accident. And as her consciousness watched, the memorial service was held around the casing containing the captain's body. Crew members took turns saying something about the captain, whether a memory or a wish that they could have said more to her. First Officer Chakotay admitted to the crew that this kind of emotional release was best to help them move on. And then, he said, "We will honor the captain one last time. Please stand."

The crew rose to attention, and the casing was released into space at the sound of the bosun's whistle.

## Change of Command

The Change of Command Ceremony is not prescribed specifically by Starfleet regulations, but rather is an honored product of the rich heritage of naval tradition. It is a custom wholly naval, without an equivalent counterpart in any other service. Custom has established that this ceremony be formal and impressive—designed to strengthen that respect for authority which is vital to any ship. Parading all hands at quarters and public reading of official orders stem from those days when movement of mail and persons was a slow process. This procedure was designated to insure that only duly authorized officers held command and that all aboard were aware of its authenticity.

The heart of the ceremony is the formal reading of official orders by the relieving officer and the officer to be relieved. Command passes upon utterance by the relieving officer, "I relieve you, sir." The officer being relieved responds, "I stand relieved." This simple procedure is duplicated hundreds of times daily throughout the ships of the Federation as each watch officer passes responsibility to his or her relief in the conduct of each ship's routine.

When Jean-Luc Picard first became the *Enterprise's* captain, all the pomp expected was evidenced. Though not the entire crew was present, all the senior staff, in accordance with tradition, was there. At the blow of the ancient bosun's whistle, the assemblage snapped to attention. Lieutenant Tasha Yar stood by. The captain read his own assignment aloud to the crew:

> "To Captain Jean-Luc Picard, Stardate 41148. You are hereby requested and required to take command of the *U.S.S. Enterprise* as of this date. Signed, Rear Admiral Norah Satie, Starfleet Command."

A quick review of those now in his command, he nodded an approval, a bosun's whistle was sounded again, and Picard announced his crew dismissed.

The ancient days of strict military assemblage and behavior are long past, but the honor and the tradition stand forth. The respect shown to the captain during the ceremony of gaining the new command or passing command to another is well deserved

and due to every Starfleet officer who has ever served on an active vessel.

When the Federation was negotiating a treaty with the Cardassian Empire, the *Enterprise* command was passed from Captain Picard to Captain Edward Jellico. With a call of "Attention to orders," the assembled crew awaited the transition. The departing captain, Picard, read the transfer:

"To Captain Jean-Luc Picard, Commanding Officer, *U.S.S. Enterprise*. Stardate 46358. You are hereby required to relinquish command of your vessel to Captain Edward Jellico, Commanding Officer, *U.S.S. Cairo,* as of this date. Signed, Vice Admiral Alynna Nechayev, Starfleet Command. Computer, transfer all command codes to Captain Edward Jellico. Voice authorization: Picard-delta-five."

The computer responded:

"Transfer complete. *U.S.S. Enterprise* now under command of Captain Edward Jellico."

A bosun's whistle was heard. The captains faced each other and repeated the time-honored words that are the heart of the ceremony. Jellico said to Picard, "I relieve you, sir."

To which Picard responded, "I stand relieved."

Picard shook Jellico's hand and the ceremony was over. The new captain turned to his crew and dismissed them.

This full ceremony isn't the norm in today's Starfleet, but a ceremony like this indicates that the changeover is likely to be more permanent than a temporary transfer, which might simply take place in the captain's wardroom, as might happen in times of war.

## Admiral's Banquet

The Admiral's Banquet is an elaborate annual function to which captains are invited. Though no one has ever said this on record, it is considered a tedious event. Many captains find ways of avoiding it, although six years of avoidance might be considered extreme.

The banquet is simply a gathering of high-ranking Starfleet officers, who discuss situations in the organization in a relaxed capacity. Relaxed, perhaps, for the admirals; the captains invited are a bit more put out. It has been described as "fifty admirals shaking hands, making dull conversation, uninteresting food, boring speeches."

## Ship's Christening

Another ancient tradition dating back to early wooden ships is the ship's christening. Commemorating the inauguration of a new ship, it holds meaning for the ship's crew.

When the *U.S.S. Enterprise* NCC-1701-B was newly commissioned, the christening was a huge affair, (2293). Media attention was extreme, and dignitaries—including the highly decorated Captain James T. Kirk, who was captain of the previous *Enterprise*—were invited to attend.

One traditional element of a ship's christening is the use of champagne. The effervescent beverage has had connections to wealth, celebrations, and romance since it was first distilled on ancient Earth. All Starfleet-commissioned ships are christened with champagne. This is done by shattering a bottle on the ship's hull, which is in accordance with the way the wooden ships of old Earth were christened.

The significance of this harkens back to ancient times, when it was thought that the spirit of the ship's sponsor would enter the ship upon christening. Much like ancient Earth religious beliefs in which water was poured over someone's head to baptize them into the religious family, the champagne represents the water of life flowing into the ship. A form of this tradition can be found across the Federation, in many different cultures.

# Weddings

## Mating Rituals and Love Connections

"On Earth, we select our own mate, someone we care for. On Earth, men and women live together, help each other, make each other happy."

—*James T. Kirk, Stardate 3211.7*

On ships, throughout history, the captains have had the honor of serving as master of ceremonies in uniting crew members in marriage.

Captain James T. Kirk is on record as having begun the following ceremony on Stardate 1709.2, but was unable to complete it, because the *Enterprise* fell under Romulan attack. The words he spoke at the time are still used in some form by all Starfleet officers given the opportunity to conduct such a ceremony:

"Since the day of the first wooden vessels, all ship masters have had one happy privilege . . . that of uniting two people in the bonds of matrimony. And so we are gathered here today, with you, Angela Martine, and you, Robert Tomlinson, in the sight of your fellows, and in accordance with our laws, and our many beliefs, that you may pledge . . ."

The Ten-Forward space of the *U.S.S. Enterprise* (NCC-1701-D) was the site chosen for many couples who were wed. When Chief Miles O'Brien married Keiko Ishikawa (2367), there was a melding

of Irish and Japanese traditions within the ceremony. The bride began the ceremony in another room praying to her ancestors. She wore a semi-traditional Japanese wedding kimono of silk, with a few modern touches.

The bride is traditionally presented to the groom by her father. In this case, Commander Data stood in. Data took a white earthenware goblet from the table and handed it to the bride. Keiko drank from it in three quick sips and then handed it to the groom who also drank in three sips. The goblet was placed back on the table. Captain Jean-Luc Picard began the ceremony:

> "Since the time of the first wooden sailing ships, all captains have enjoyed the happy privilege of joining two people in the bonds of matrimony. And so now it is my honor to unite you, Keiko Ishikawa, and you, Miles Edward O'Brien, together in marriage here in the sight of your friends and family."

Captain Benjamin Sisko was wed to freighter captain Kasidy Yates on board Deep Space 9 (2375). Though he admits that the Bajoran Prophets have warned him not to wed, Sisko is able to follow his heart and organize a shipboard wedding. Admiral William Ross presided.

> "One of the most pleasant duties of a senior officer is the privilege of joining two people together in matrimony. Today it is my honor to unite Kasidy Shameeka Yates and Benjamin Lafayette Sisko in marriage.

"Kasidy, do you accept this man as your husband, to love and cherish above all others, until death separates you?"

The bride replied, "I do."
Admiral Ross asked:

"Benjamin, do you accept this woman as your wife, to love and cherish, above all others, until death separates you?"

The groom replied, "I do."

Once again, the admiral continued:

"These rings symbolize your love for each other, and your promise to abide by the vows you've made today."

In turn, the pair replied, "With this ring, I thee wed."

"By the power invested in me, by the United Federation of Planets, I pronounce you husband and wife."

*Voyager*'s status didn't suspend the natural course of shipboard life. In all things, whenever there was the chance to boost morale, the crew went all out. What was once the captain's mess was remade into a working kitchen to fix meals for the crew. The new mess hall became the center of off-duty functions. It even served as a makeshift wedding chapel.

This ceremony incorporates the ancient Earth custom of throwing uncooked rice at the bride and groom. The idea is to shower the newlyweds with a symbol of good fortune.

B'Elanna Torres and Tom Paris were married while *Voyager* was in the Delta Quadrant. However, the record of the ceremony was lost due to damage suffered by the ship's memory core during *Voyager*'s passage through the Borg transwarp aperture. The following account has been pieced together by the crew.

Keeping with tradition, Captain Kathryn Janeway performed the ceremony, allowing for adaptation to the traditional:

"We're gathered here today—not as Starfleet officers, but as friends and family—to celebrate the marriage of two of *Voyager*'s finest. B'Elanna's asked me to forgo the rigors of Klingon painsticks in favor of a more traditional ceremony.

"As captain, the honor of joining these two people has fallen to me. Before I declare them husband and wife, Tom and B'Elanna have prepared their own vows."

Lieutenant Tom Paris spoke first:

"I'm still not sure what I've done to deserve you. But whatever it is, I'll try to keep doing it. I promise to stand by you and to honor you till death do us part."

Ensign Harry Kim, standing as best man, produced a simple gold band and handed it to Paris, who slipped it on Torres's finger. He said:

"May this ring be a symbol of our eternal love."

Chief Engineer Torres then said:

"You stood by me when most people would've run for the airlock. You were willing to see past my shortcomings with all the bumps and bruises along the way. You made me a better person . . . even though I put up one hell of a fight.

"I look forward to our journey ahead."

Chakotay, standing up for Torres, handed her a ring. She then repeated:

"May this ring be a symbol of our eternal love."

Janeway then announced:

"Lieutenant Thomas Eugene Paris, Lieutenant
B'Elanna Torres, with the power vested in me by
Starfleet Command and the United Federation of
Planets, I now pronounce you husband and wife."

Weddings have been an important part of Starfleet, not just in
joining officers together but as a way to broaden cultural acceptance. Moments of political stress have occurred when non-
Federation planets look to cease their hostilities by marrying two
of their own. There are life-forms who are bred to serve as gifts of
marriage, bonding themselves to their intended for the good of
their people. The Federation doesn't look highly upon these practices, seeing it as a form of slavery, but they respect the practices
of non-Federation planets and encourage the understanding of
more equal ways of bonding.

# TWO

*Klingons*

Proud and honor-bound, the Klingon people have a bloody but glorious history. If a Klingon gives you his word, it's good for generations. Honor is the undisputed foundation of the Klingon Empire.

All Klingons, men and women, are warriors and will fight for the honor of the Empire. Worf, son of Mogh, later of the House of Martok, was the first Klingon warrior to serve in Starfleet. He now stands as Federation ambassador to Qo'noS, and exemplifies that warrior spirit. Worf could have served as chancellor, but his honor told him that Martok would better lead the Klingon Empire, and Worf stepped aside.

Male and female Klingons serve in the Klingon Defense Force, but women are not allowed to serve on the High Council. Females are responsible for the upkeep and preservation of the traditions and lore of their families and House, approving of betrothed, welcoming new members of the House, and defending those same traditions when necessary.

Loud and boisterous, Klingons know how to live every day as if it were their last. If death awaits them on that day, they embrace that as well.

## Age of Ascension

One of the most important celebrations in the life of any Klingon warrior is the Age of Ascension. The Age of Ascension is a rite of initiation, marking a new level of Klingon spiritual attainment.

> *DaHjaj Duvwl"e' jlH*
> *tlqwlj Sa'angnlS.*
> *'Iw blQtlqDaq jljaH.*

In Standard:

>Today I am a warrior.
>I must show you my heart.
>I travel the river of blood.

With the reciting of these lines in Klingonese, the young Klingon warrior acknowledges the attainment of a certain spiritual level. The new warrior then proceeds to walk the gauntlet of painstiks. The Klingon traditions are emphasized in this ritual.

>*YIn DayajmeH 'oy' yISIQ*

and

>*'oy'naQ Dalo'be'chugh not nenghep lop puq.*

translate as:

>To understand life, endure pain.

As time passes, a child inevitably becomes an adult. What is not inevitable is that an adult becomes a warrior. A warrior must be forged like a sword, tempered by experience. The path of the warrior begins with the first Rite of Ascension.

A young Klingon's fighting skills are tested, as well as his knowledge of the teachings of Kahless. A *kor'tova* candle is lit, representing the fire that burns in a warrior's heart and declaring his intention of becoming warrior. If he does not participate in the rite before thirteen years of age, a Klingon boy will never be able to become a true Klingon warrior.

The Second Rite of Ascension puts the warrior through the challenge of the painstiks, which is reenacted on the anniversary of the Age of Ascension.

The celebration takes place in a large chamber that's eerily lit, with walls and floors made of polished stainless steel. There's a wide trough in the middle that runs into a drain. There are platforms on either side of the trough. Eight Klingons stand on each side of the trough, each holding a painstik.

The celebrating Klingon recites the traditional *DaHjaj Suvwl''e' jlH. Tlgwlj Sa'SangNIS, 'lw blQtlqDaq jljaH.*

It is noted that the true test of Klingon strength is to admit one's most profound feelings while under extreme duress. What is said is personal, but at Worf's Ascension anniversary he was found to say:

> *jlbechrup may'vllos.*

The first two Klingons jab the participant with the painstiks as he walks down the corridor. In his instant, Worf writhed in agony, but he continued, his growl weaker:

> The battle is mine. I crave only the blood of the enemy.

He continued to the next pair of Klingons, and said:

> *HlHlvqa'*

More painstiks are utilized, and Worf said:

> The bile of the vanquished flows over my hands.

The last set of warriors administer their painstiks, to which Worf replied:

> *may'pequ' moH.*

The warrior may react in different ways. However, to fall to his knees and twitch violently is the desired effect. Klingons are

most enthusiastic following this ritual. Within their culture, the yearly anniversary of the Age of Ascension is celebrated by a warrior with his friends and family administering the painstiks, helping him re-create the day he acknowledged the warrior within.

## Day of Honor

Testing one's honor by enduring a traditional ritual ordeal and examining behavior over the last year to see if one measures up to Klingon standards is the main focus of the Day of Honor. A Klingon warrior first feasts on *targ* and drinks *mot'lock* from a ritual Grail of Kahless. The Ritual of Twenty Painstiks precedes a fight with a *bat'leth* master and traversing the sulfur lagoons of Gorath.

The Klingon interrogator waits for the participant and asks a series of questions:

> *Qu'pla!* What warrior goes there?
>
> Have you come to have your honor challenged?
>
> Are you willing to see the ceremony through to the end?

After receiving the proper answers, the interrogator continues:

> It will be a lengthy ordeal. First, you must eat from the heart of a sanctified *targ*. The heart of the *targ* brings courage to one who eats it. Next, you will drink *mot'loch* from the Grail of Kahless. Drink to the glory of Kahless, the greatest warrior of all time. Kahless defeated his enemies on the field of battle and built a mighty empire. How have you proven yourself worthy?

After the interrogator gets the answers he's looking for, the ceremony continues:

> A warrior must endure great hardship. To test your mettle you will endure the Ritual of Twenty Painstiks. After that you will engage in combat with a master of the *bat'leth*. Finally, you will traverse the sulfur lagoons of Gorath.

Once a Klingon warrior has successfully completed these tasks, he has reclaimed and proven his honor.

## Tea Ceremony

Don't let the name fool you: the Klingon tea ceremony has very specific, warriorlike symbolism. The statement

*Heghly'DI' mobbe'lu'chugh QaQqu' Hegh wanI'*

translates as:

**Death is an experience best shared.**

Two friends share poisoned tea to test their bravery and prove the above quote. Paying tribute to warriors who battle side by side as well as to the dignity of death in battle, the Klingon tea ceremony takes place during times between wars to reinforce the central warlike nature of the honor-bound Klingons.

A tray set with two delicate, spartan cups, a stone teapot, and a thorn-covered branch with a single blossom midway up the branch is needed for the tea ceremony. One participant strips several of the thorns from the branch and tosses them into the steaming pot. The other participant plucks off the white blossom and places it in one of the cups so that the tea pours through the petals.

The Klingon tea ceremony is a test of bravery, of one's ability to look at the face of mortality. It is also a reminder that death is an experience best shared—like the tea.

## *R'uustai*

Resplendent in Klingon ceremony is *R'uustai,* the rite in which two people bond to become siblings. The ceremony includes lighting of ceremonial candles, wearing warrior's sashes, and honoring mothers with a Klingon intonation:

> You will become part of my family now and for all
> time. We will be brothers.

The room is dark, and five intricate Klingon candles are on tables in the background; only one is lit. Each Klingon removes his familial sash and places it across the other's shoulders. Each takes a candle and walks to the lit candle, lighting the one he holds. As they go around and light the others, the instigator of the ceremony says:

> *Sos jIH batlh Soh,*

which honors the memory of their mothers and bonds the two. Their families are now stronger.

## *Hegh'bat* and *Mauk-to' Vor*

Suicide is looked upon as dishonorable behavior in Klingon society, but there are instances when a form of assisted suicide is acceptable.

*Hegh'bat* literally means "the time to die," and it is the chosen method of death when a Klingon warrior cannot stand and face his enemies—usually due to a grave injury. The warrior refuses to be an object of pity or a burden to his family and friends. In this ritual, a family member—preferably the eldest son—or a trusted friend delivers a ritual knife to the warrior, who then impales himself on it.

*Mauk-to'Vor* is the ritualistic killing of a dishonored warrior by the one who caused the dishonor, thus restoring the deceased's honor. With candles burning and a small shrine set up, the two warriors prepare for the ritual. As the dishonored prays, the other warrior waves *adanjy* incense over his subject's head.

The intended speaks:

> You have been wronged in this life. There is nothing
> left here for you. No honor. No future.

The dishonored replies:

> I wish to reclaim my honor in the next life . . . I am ready to cross the river of blood to enter *Sto-Vo-Kor*.

The intended holds the *mevak* knife, saying:

> Let this blade speed you on your journey.

The dishonored rips his clothing to expose his chest, and the intended plunges the knife into him, thus allowing him to die with honor.

## Right of Vengeance

The Right of Vengeance is highly respected because

> *bortaS nIvqu' 'oH bortaS'e'.*

meaning, in Standard:

> Revenge is the best revenge.

Aside from the acceptable warrior slant, the Right of Vengeance has legal standing especially in regards to dishonor. If someone wrongs your family, you are given the opportunity to enact the Right of Vengeance, which can be handled by the chancellor offering you the life of the Klingon who has wronged you.

Worf was given that option by Gowron to redeem his family honor by killing a member of the House of Duras. He turned it down because it went against Starfleet regulations, but he explained, "I will not kill him for the crimes of his family."

His brother, Kurn, did not appreciate Worf turning down the Right, believing that honor was not properly restored. Kurn believed, "A Klingon who denies himself the Right of Vengeance is no Klingon at all."

## *Bat'leth* Competition

The *Bat'leth* Competition is an annual Klingon martial-arts festival celebrating the Sword of Honor. On one occasion, Worf took leave from the *Enterprise* to participate, and he attained champion standing.

Fighting is an art form among Klingons; this competition displays various techniques practiced by the warriors. Since the knowledge and history of all things Klingon are also vital to them, the competition is not just about fighting. It also honors Kahless and remembers his forging the first *bat'leth*.

## Weddings

When it comes to romance, Klingon men do not roar. In fact, in the matters of Klingon love, the women roar and throw heavy objects, and they tend to claw at the men. The men, in this teaming of *par'machkai*—romantic partners—tend to read poetry . . . while ducking a lot.

Klingon women are partners in battle to the men, but they also are the mothers to the children, and all the natural oxymoronic tendencies that go along with that. *Par'Mach* means "love" and has more aggressive overtones than what many other humanoid cultures may understand. Klingons live life with aggression, and they love with nothing less than their entire warrior spirit.

## Informal Wedding

One particular line of Klingon poetry,

*bomDI' 'IwwIj qaqaw,*

translated to:

The memory of you sings in my blood.

shows the lyrical response in memory triggering. The line sounds as if the blood's song concerns the object of affection. In fact, the ancient words of devotion focus on the mingling of blood: "*jIH dok*" (my blood) to which is responded "*maj dok*" (our blood).

The informal marriage arrangements, which are usually preceded by a physical union, are uncommon in present time, though not unheard of. The man stands up, looking skyward, and proclaims:

*tlhIngan jIH,*

which roughly translates to:

I am a Klingon.

The woman states the same, and then the two solemnize their union with the oath and pledge that they are one forever, since Klingons mate for life. They need no one else present, merely the intention to be together suffices.

## Formal Wedding Rituals

The more formal marriage arrangement is resplendent, the way one might expect a Klingon wedding to be. With a warrior's tale of how the first Klingon hearts were forged, the two are joined forever; they have embarked on a spiritual journey that will bind them together through their present life and the next. The mistress of the House that the female is joining is usually the one to perform the ceremony. However, this is only if the mistress approves of the bride and after she has passed through the *Bre'Nan* ritual.

In the *Bre'Nan* ritual, the mistress tests the bride-to-be, passing judgment on the warrior's choice. It is a Klingon trial: it is not easy.

The prospective bride welcomes the mistress of the House she intends to enter by greeting her, saying:

*Tug son bosh mok A'Beh koh. E'gagh vet moh.*

Translated into Standard:

Enter my home and be welcome, Mistress. May you find it worthy.

The mistress replies:

*Eck'taH roh masa qee'Plok,*

meaning:

May this be the first of many visits.

The bride-to-be is required to have authentic *var'Hama* candles, which are made by slaughtering three captured *targs* in a ritual sacrifice, boiling their shoulders into tallow, and spending two days molding them into candles by hand.

The mistress of the House explains that the bride's worthiness to join the House is judged according to the traditions of her family, beginning with the ritual meal.

Following the meal, the bride-to-be is subjected to a specific ritual where she must recite a prayer to Kahless while holding two heavy braziers full of burning embers; at the same time, she slowly revolves with her arms held straight out to her side. She says:

Ko'ma tlang'goS. ak-bay
Hava'dak crossh tovah
Ko'ma Kahless. Ko'ma Kahless. Ko'na Kahless
Al'Qoch mesah t'lang cho.

She completes the ritual by perfectly placing the brazier on two Klingon columns. After the completion of this test, the intended is required to recite the complete chronicle of the women in the mistress's family.

While the women conduct their ceremony, the groom and his closest male friends begin the *Kal'Hyah* four days before the wedding. The *Kal'Hyah* is the path of clarity and is considered a great journey. This is similar to the Earth custom of the bachelor party, but only in the specifics of the men getting together before the wedding. The *Kal'Hyah* takes place in Klingon caverns, decorated with hieroglyphics, iron torches, a table with a full Klingon feast, and a large fire pit that makes the room stifling hot. Preparing for the journey, the guests are handed *Ma'Stakas*, which will be used to attack the couple at the conclusion of the wedding ceremony. This tradition dates back to the wedding of Kahless and Lukara, who were nearly killed by Molor's troops moments after they were married. The clubs are carried by the men until the ceremony.

There are six trials on the path to *Kal'Hyah:* deprivation, blood, pain, sacrifice, anguish, and death. The food is used in the first trial—deprivation—in order to tempt the participants into break-

ing the fast. The whole point of the *Kal'Hyah* journey is to push the limits of one's endurance.

Klingons tend to sing in situations like this. The *Kal'Hyah* song, in Klingon:

*Kaaa vek ko lee ko*
*Eh to che mah to*
*Tah oo-wah kah esh to pah deh ah reee!*
*Yah bosh-ah!*
*Yah bosh-ah!*
*Ya bosh tomah!*

In the trial of blood, the men stand in a semicircle while the groom sharpens a long curved sword with barbed and serrated edges. He says:

Now begins the trial of blood . . .
Let rivers flow from our veins . . .
And stain the ground with our sacrifice . . .

A volunteer steps forward to be the first to sacrifice a portion of himself.

When Worf and Jadzia Dax decided to get married, they chose Deep Space 9 as the locale to accommodate friends and family. This allowed Worf to have his son, Alexander Rozhenko, as *Tawi'Yan* (sword-bearer, or Klingon best man).

## Vows

Klingon drums are played. As the mistress of the House begins the ceremony, everyone falls silent.

"With fire and steel did the gods forge the Klingon heart. So fiercely did it beat, so loud was the sound, that the gods cried out, "On this day we have brought forth the strongest heart in all the heavens. None can stand before it without trembling at its strength." But then the Klingon heart weakened, its steady rhythm faltered, and the gods said, "Why do you weaken so? We have made you the strongest in all of creation." And the heart said . . ."

The groom steps up to the mistress and responds:

"I . . . am alone."

The mistress continues:

"And the gods knew that they had erred. So they went back to their forge and brought forth another heart."

The bride enters and joins the groom, facing him. The *Tawi'Yan*—sword-bearer—steps forward, and the couple each take a *bat'leth* from him. As the mistress tells all:

"But the second heart beat stronger than the first, and the first was jealous of its power."

The groom swings his *bat'leth* at the bride, but she parries and gets her blade up to his neck.

At that instant the mistress reminds the bride:

"Fortunately, the second heart was tempered by wisdom."

And the bride replies:

"If we join together, no forces can stop us."

The bride takes her blade away from her groom's neck, and the two pull each other close, with their faces almost touching. The mistress continues.

"And when the two hearts began to beat together, they filled the heavens with a terrible sound. For the first time, the gods knew fear. They tried to flee, but it was too late.

"The Klingon hearts destroyed the gods who created them and turned the heavens to ashes. To this very day, no one can oppose the beating of two Klingon hearts. Does your heart beat only for this woman?"

48

The groom states an affirmative. The ceremony continues.

"And will you swear to join with her and stand with her against all who oppose you?"

He agrees again, and she continues, turning to the bride, asking the same questions:

"Does your heart beat only for this man? And do you swear to join with him and stand with him against all who would oppose you?"

The bride stands in agreement, and in conclusion, spoken to all is:

"Then let all present here today know that this man and this woman are married."

This ends the speaking of the vows. The Klingon drums begin again as the couple kisses. Then the men who joined the groom in the *Kal'Hyah* rush the platform carrying *ma'Stakas* to attack the newly married couple and instigate the traditional Klingon wedding congratulations.

## Death Rituals

Klingon death rituals celebrate the successful life of a warrior. They do not grieve the loss of the body but celebrate the releasing of the spirit. Many Klingon maxims focus on the inevitability of death, including,

*bogh tlhInganpu', SuvwI'pu' moj, Hegh,*

which translates to:

Klingons are born, live as warriors, then die.

And, of course, the very basic

*Heghlu'meH QaQ jajvam,*

which means:

It is a good day to die.

And of course,

*Batlh blHeghjaj,*

meaning:

May you die well.

## Death Chant

For a Klingon, when a friend has died in battle, it is a joyful time. The Klingon death chant sings the praises of the fallen. In Klingon, the chant is:

*nelt talk Qo'noS.*
*Heg bat'lhgu Hoch nej malt.*
*nelt talt Qo'noS.*
*yay je bat'lh manob Hegh.*

translated into Standard:

Only Kronos endures.
All we can hope for is a glorious death.
Only Kronos endures.
In death there is victory and honor.

## Death Howl

After prying open the eyes of the fallen, a Klingon death howl—an exaltation of the victorious—goes up upon the passing of a war-

rior, as a warning to the dead in *Sto-Vo-Kor* that a warrior is soon to be among them. Klingons traditionally unceremoniously discard the body as an empty shell once the cry goes up, for it is the spirit that is the focus. At other times, however, a funereal dirge may be sung in honor of the deceased. It is a sacred text that has never been officially translated into Standard:

*Ki-naH-naH, lo-maytoo;*
*Ki-nah-nah; lo-maytoH;*
*ko-no-ma. . .ko-no-mayy*

## Ak'voh

This is the Klingon tradition of staying with a fallen warrior after death to keep predators away; it is accompanied by the death howl. The belief that the body is just the vessel and the spirit is what's important is emphasized here, for

*HeghDI' SuvwI' nargh SuvwI' qa',*

which means:

When a warrior dies, his spirit escapes.

Comrades staying by the body to keep it safe give the spirit the time it needs to leave and begin the long journey to *Sto-Vo-Kor.*

## Sto-Vo-Kor

Victory over all and victory in death allow a warrior to enter *Sto-Vo-Kor,* the place in the Klingon afterlife for honored dead (much like Valhalla in ancient Earth Norse mythology). Klingon tradition calls for a warrior to have eaten the heart of an enemy as well as

to have died in glorious battle. It is said that Kahless awaits the warriors who enter *Sto-Vo-Kor*.

Following the death of his wife Jadzia Dax, Worf takes on a dangerous mission and dedicates it to her memory. Since she was a warrior who did not die in battle, Klingon tradition demanded that he risk his life in her name in order for her to enter *Sto-Vo-Kor*. The crew chanted:

*Vond Shoo-vwee Dun Mahh-Kekk Huh-Kov-Vahm*
*Jeh Yin-Moj Mah-Mukh.*
*Sto-ve-kor Pah-Dahkh-tin Baht-leh*
*el-eegh-cha yay-moj.*

which is translated to:

We dedicate this mission and our lives to the
memory of a great warrior.
Through our victory, she will enter the sacred halls
of *Sto-Vo-Kor*.

The crew then shed their own blood by slicing their hand with a long *d'k tahg* and anointed the ship's bulkhead with the blood, reciting:

*YuWee-modge. Baht-leh-modge. Yah Dodge.*
*Lohn-Ict-lihj push-Mochh-ludge Sto-Ko-Vor,*

which is translated to:

Blood. Honor. Glory.
Open your gates, *Sto-Vo-Kor*.

Another legend associated with *Sto-Vo-Kor* is that of the Cursed. Dishonored souls are taken to Gre'thor on the Barge of the Dead. Gre'thor is protected by Fek'lhr, a mythical beast that is similar to a devil of ancient Earth lore, although it has been said that Klingons have no devil in their mythology. Protecting the land of the dead is more akin to the role Cerebus had in the ancient Greek culture of old Earth.

The sins of the child may send a parent to Gre'thor. If a child turns its back on Klingon ways, the parent must pay the price when he dies.

The eleventh tome of Klavek tells a story about Kahless returning from the dead. He was "still bearing a wound from the afterlife . . ." as a warning that what he experienced wasn't a dream. Kahless had traveled to the afterlife to rescue his brother from the Barge of the Dead and deliver him to *Sto-Vo-Kor*.

# Political

## Joining a House

Being a member of a House is an important indication in Klingon culture. Members of Klingon Houses are awarded seats on the Council and all the rights that go along with that. But a House can fall if its members are not honorable, as was the case with the House of Duras. Worf's House lost its standing during the Dominion War. It was only when Martok saw that Worf was a warrior of honor that he asked Worf to join the House of Martok. The members of a House usually wear a symbol of that House on their clothing.

It is also customary for brides to present their *d'h tagh* (dagger) to the master of the House as a formal request that they be accepted into the new House.

The more formal admittance into a House is an ancient cere-mony. A wooden box decorated with Klingon writing, a golden bowl, a jeweled decanter, and a ceremonial candle are laid out. The crest of the House is held over a shallow golden bowl; candles reflect in the sides of the bowl. This is the formal ritual used by the House of Martok:

*Martok degh, to-Duj, bat-leh degh, mat-leh degh,*

or:

Badge of Martok, badge of courage, badge of honor, badge of loyalty.

The crest is placed in the bowl, and they say:

*Martok degh,*

meaning:

Badge of Martok.

The initiate then gives his dagger to the master, who slices into his palm, closes his fist, and drips his blood onto the crest, saying:

*Wachk ihw, wachk kkor-duh,*

meaning:

One blood, one house.

All present do the same, with the initiate going last.

The master of the House then covers the crest with liquid from the decanter and touches the candle flame to it. The bowl bursts into flame.

The initiate then proclaims:

*Mat-leh gih-Hegh!*

translated to mean:

I will be faithful even beyond death!

The fire burns out, and the master says, "*Dah!*" (Now!) and the initiate reaches into the bowl, pulls out the crest, and places it on his shoulder.

The initiate is then welcomed into the House.

## *Brek'tal* Ritual

The *brek'tal* ritual is a very particular rite, wherein following slaying the head of a House in honorable combat, the victor takes the victim's place as the new head of the House.

Grabbing one of the victor's hands, the widow speaks formally:

*Go'Eveh . . . lu cha wabeh . . . Mo ka re'chos.*

The man replies:

*Go'Eveh . . . lu cha wabeh . . . to va re'Luk.*

The simple ceremony is complete, and the two are joined as husband and wife.

Grilka presented her new husband to the Council. They were shocked, but she informed them, "All I have done is follow the *brek'tal* ritual. If the leader of a House is slain in honorable combat, the victor may be invited to take his place . . . and his wife."

This ritual may be practiced to keep the House whole or away from an unsuitable (or dishonorable) brother, who would have claimant rights over ruling the House once the older brother has been killed.

## Divorce

A Klingon divorce is very simple. If the man asks for one, the woman backhands him and snarls over him:

*N'Gos tlhogh cha!*

meaning:

Our marriage is done!

She then spits on him, and they are separated.

## Discommendation

An individual who receives discommendation is treated as nonexistent in the eyes of Klingon society. The individual's family is also disgraced for seven generations. Worf accepted a humiliating discommendation based on his late father's apparent treason at Khitomer. Standing with his *cha-DIch* (an ancient Earth term would be "your second"), the accused hears the full accusation. After a full hearing and *mek'ba*, the presentation of the evidence, was completed in Worf's case, instead of challenging the accusation, he took on discommendation. Worf stood before the Council and stated:

*tlhIH ghItj jIH yoj,*

meaning:

I fear your judgment.

The Council leader replied:

*biHunch,*

which means:

Coward.

The crowd assembled reacts with disgust. Then the full Council rises and, as one, turns their back on the accused. The crowd then does the same. And the accused and his *cha-DIch* leave the presence of the Council.

This discommendation of the House of Mogh was later reversed by Gowron. He stated, "You both [Worf and his brother, Kurn] fought as warriors; you have proved your hearts are Klingon."

Pulling out his *d'k tahg,* Gowron offered the blade to Worf, who took it firmly in his hand until blood dripped out. Gowron announced:

> "I return your family honor. I give you back what was
> wrongfully taken from you. Let your name be spoken
> once again. You are Worf, son of Mogh."

## *Kot'baval* Festival

The *Kot'baval* Festival is the traditional celebration of the ancient victory of Kahless the Unforgettable.

A Klingon street opera is usually performed in the town center. Two Klingons are singing and engaging in mock combat, accompanied by musicians who are making a din only a Klingon could love. The performers are clad in elaborate colorful robes; their *bat'leth* swords have bells attached that jingle when they fight.

One performer represents Molor. He is so strong that no one can stand against him. The fallen performer sings plaintively:

> *Nok'tar be'got, hosh'ar te'not . . . ?*

Which is him asking if anyone else will have the courage to stand up to Molor.

They look around for the new challenger, and the singer asks again:

*Nok'tar be'got . . . ?*

Another challenger steps forward to accept:

*Ki'rok Molor, ki'rok!*

Molor springs forth to attack and cries out:

*Ni'tokr bak'to!*

They continue to fight and sing. Molor speaks out:

*Ba'jak ta'mo!*

His opponent responds defiantly:

*O'tak ta'ro!*

They spar some more, but the opponent falls, looking to the audience and asking who will save them from Molor:

*Nok'tar be'got?*

Molor sings in triumph as the crowd hisses. But only one man can stand against Molor, and when the first singer comes back in a different costume, the crowd cheers because Kahless has arrived.

Kahless rears himself up and sings:

*Nok'til Kahless. Molor kgik'tal!*

The crowd roars back in approval, because Kahless would rather die than live under Molor's tyranny.

## Officer Succession

In Klingon tradition, when an officer is looked upon as being unfit to serve, the next in command challenges him to a battle to the death. If it was the commander of a vessel, the officer would announce:

> "As first officer, I say you are unfit to serve as captain. You are a coward, and I challenge you for command of this ship."

They then fight, and the victor is ship's captain.

## Rite of Succession

In choosing a new leader for the Klingon High Council, the Rite of Succession is used. Once the *Sonchi* rite is completed, and the former leader is officially pronounced dead, the Arbiter of Succession is called in. Captain Jean-Luc Picard stood as Arbiter of Succession when a replacement for K'mpec was required, choosing the challengers for the Council's leadership. The two strongest challengers would then fight. Picard reintroduced *ja'chuq*, an obsolete ceremony in which the challengers list their accomplishments to establish their worthiness.

Once K'mpec died, a Klingon "wake" was performed before the Rite of Succession could take place. K'mpec's corpse was accorded no reverence; it had been left sitting in his chair. The two challengers to the High Council seat participated, as did the Arbiter who approached the body and challenged:

> *Qab . . . jIH . . . nagil!*

which means:

> Face me if you dare!

He placed the end of the painstik onto K'mpec's chest. The challengers followed in the same act. K'Ehleyr announced:

> *Sonchi.*

which proclaimed:

> He is dead.

The Rite of Succession is a long, involved ceremony in which the challengers list the battles they've won and the praises they've accumulated. The idea is to prove their worthiness to lead the Council.

The Klingon representative, K'Tal, noted, "Gowron, son of M'Rel, *hakt'em,* the Arbiter confirms that you have completed the Rite of Succession. Your enemies have been destroyed; you stand alone. Do you want to claim leadership of the Council?"

Gowron said yes and, with no other challengers, K'Tal said: "Receive now the loyalty of the Council and of the Empire."

The chancellor's cloak was placed upon the new leader's shoulders, and he stepped up to the leader's chair. He turned and faced them and announced, "Let all who have opposed me now swear loyalty or die with shame."

Everyone replied, "*Qapla!*"

Which is the traditional Klingon salute of success.


During the Dominion War, Gowron's leadership of the High Council was challenged because it was believed that he was putting his personal interests ahead of the good of the Empire.

Worf proclaimed to Gowron, thereby challenging his rule, "You rule without wisdom and without honor. The warriors gathered here will not say this to you, but I will. You are squandering our ships and our lives in a petty act of vengeance. You do not care what happens to the Empire; you only care about Gowron. What I say now, I say as a member of the House of Martok, not as a Starfleet officer: You have dishonored yourself and the Empire. You are not worthy of leading the Council."

This verbal challenge was met physically with *bat'leths.* It was a close and brutal fight. They both did damage, but Worf

was victorious. He leaned over the dead Gowron, prying open his eyes, and gave the traditional death howl. Martok moved to put the chancellor's cloak on Worf and proclaimed:

Hail Worf! Leader of the Empire!

But Worf turned down the position, quoting Kahless:

Great men do not seek power; they have power thrust up on them.

And he turned and put the cloak on Martok's shoulders.

Hail Martok! Leader of the Empire! Leader of destiny!

# THREE

# Vulcans

Peace and long life
Live long and prosper

With these greetings, the Vulcans sum up what they believe.

The philosophy of the Vulcans is to celebrate the beauty to be found in the spectacular variety of the universe, but logic reigns supreme. Vulcans are logical and unemotional; any showing of emotions is simply not done. Because they are also telepathic they prefer to avoid having physical contact with other life-forms. They are a private people, almost to the point of being aloof, but their lives and their traditions are central to everything they are.

## Rumarie

*Rumarie* is an ancient Vulcan pagan festival that has not been celebrated for a millennium. It goes back to a time before Vulcans embraced logic. It is "full of barely clothed Vulcan men and women, covered with slippery Rillan grease, chasing one another."

As an effort to lighten up the strain on the *Starship Voyager*, Morale Officer Neelix considers *Rumarie* as "a theme for the mess hall next week, lots of high fat, greasy foods; and if people want to take off their clothes and chase each other, it certainly wouldn't hurt morale around here."

## Time of Awakening

This is the time when the Vulcans began to move toward peace and logic, turning their backs on what they considered primitive. These are the philosophies of Surak, who led the Vulcans away from their warlike ways. The legendary Stone of Gol was pivotal during that time. According to Vulcan mythology, whoever possessed the stone need only *think* of throwing it at someone . . . and that person would be killed.

## *T'san s'at*

Like many Vulcan rituals, *t'san s'at* is a process of controlling emotions. Specifically, it is the intellectual deconstruction of emotional patterns.

Commander Tuvok explained that it is a lifelong process of study that Vulcans undertake. Harry Kim wanted to learn it to overcome a period of extreme emotion.

As Tuvok explained, "You are experiencing '*shon-ha'lock*'—the engulfment. The most intense and psychologically perilous form of Eros.

"I believe humans call it 'love at first sight.'"

## Falor's Journey

"Falor's Journey" is a traditional Vulcan folk song of one man's enlightenment. It consists of 348 verses, although it isn't necessary to sing all 348 verses.

One sample verse is as follows:

Falor was a prosperous merchant, who went on a
journey to gain greater awareness.
Through storms he crossed the Voroth Sea to
reach the clouded shores of Raal.
Where old T'Para offered truth.
He traveled through the windswept hills, across
the barren fire Plains,

to find the silent monks of Kir.
Still unfulfilled, he journeyed home, told stories of
the lessons learned,
and gained true wisdom by the giving.

# Mind-Meld

The mind-meld is an ancient Vulcan ritual that is extremely intimate and personal. It connects the participants in such a way that they share a consciousness. The mind-meld can be used to gain an understanding of another being, to help another develop a skill, or to find the truth behind a madness. The meld can also assist one in calming oneself, though the other participant may be deluged by emotions. Captain Picard was subject to a mind-meld with Ambassador Sarek, and the emotions kept in check by the Vulcan were unleashed through the human.

Prior to Sarek's death (2368) his wife Perrin noted to Picard, "You are a part of him . . . and he of you."

The mind-meld is a continuation of the Vulcan desire for logic in all things. To find the truth, you need to go into someone's mind.

"Do you know what a mind-meld is?" Tuvok asked the imprisoned Suder. "We would be telepathically linked, exchanging our thoughts, in essence becoming one mind.

"It is not without risk. But as a Vulcan, I have internal processes that allow me to control violent instincts. I believe I will be able to suppress whatever feelings I draw from you."

Tuvok reached out to Suder's face and said, "My mind to your mind, your thoughts to my thoughts . . ."

## *Kolinahr*

The *Kolinahr* is the Vulcan ritual of emotional purge, a rigorous discipline utilized to allow one to achieve a state of pure and total logic. This is a highly respected goal but a very difficult one to master. Any form of natural emotional reaction can cause a Vulcan to leave the discipline. Both Spock and Tuvok entered into a study of the *Kolinahr*. Both were forced to leave; Spock when his human side was touched by the call of the space probe V'Ger (2270); and Tuvok when he entered the *Pon farr* (2304). Tuvok did learn some of the lessons of the *Kolinahr* and practiced it.

"A house cannot stand without a foundation . . . logic is the foundation of control. . . ."

"Control is the essence of function," Tuvok recited. "I am in control . . ."

Tuvok worked on a structure called *Keethera,* a "structure of harmony." It is a meditational aid, helping Vulcans focus thought and mental control.

## *Kal Rekk*

A traditional period of atonement, solitude, and silence, it lasts only one day.

Neelix approached Tuvok. "Happy *Kal Rekk,* Mr. Vulcan."

"The holiday of *Kal Rekk* is not for two weeks," Tuvok corrected him.

"But it's the *Kal Rekk* season," the party-happy Neelix suggested.

"There is no *Kal Rekk* season. *Kal Rekk* is a day of atonement, solitude, and silence," Tuvok told him.

"Atonement, solitude, all your Vulcan holidays are the same! I've been doing some research; I know," Neelix continued.

## Koon-ut so'lik

*Koon-ut so'lik* is the ritual Vulcan marriage proposal, when a male Vulcan declares the desire to take a mate during *Pon farr.*

"We're done here," Torres told the Vulcan engineer Vorik, after they finished their assignment.

"Then let me take this opportunity to declare *koon-ut so'lik*—my desire to become your mate," Vorik told her.

"What?"

He was as calm as only a Vulcan could be. "In human terms, I am 'proposing marriage.' Do you accept?"

"This is a little sudden," she noted, "isn't it? Besides, I thought Vulcan marriages were arranged. Don't you already have someone back home?"

"She has sufficient reason to consider me lost and has most likely chosen another mate," he explained. "It's appropriate for me to do the same. I have come to greatly admire not only your impressive technical skills but also your bravery and sense of moral duty. All excellent qualities in a prospective mate."

"But you're Vulcan, I'm half Klingon," she said. "I can't imagine . . ."

This is something he can see through. "Perhaps we're not an obvious match. However, our differences could complement each other. You've often expressed frustrations with your Klingon temper. My mental discipline could help you control it.

"I should also remind you that many humanoid species are unable to withstand Klingon mating practices . . ."

Torres had to interject on this one, "Okay, that's enough."

But he wasn't done. " . . . whereas my superior Vulcan strength would make me a very suitable partner."

## *Pon farr*

*Pon farr* is the "time of mating." Every seven years, Vulcans are overcome by the natural instinct to take a mate. This can be fatal, though, if a Vulcan is unable to find a suitable mate, because a neurochemical imbalance is triggered during the *Pon farr*. The mind-meld between betrothed Vulcans draws them irresistibly to each other at this time.

"The burning of his Vulcan blood, *Pon farr*. Vulcan males must endure it every seven years of their adult life," Saavik says, explaining what the regenerated Spock is going through (2285).

"It is called *Pon farr*," she told the anguished young Spock.

"Will you trust me?" she asks him in Vulcan. She then begins the ritual with him, and he picks up the physical procedure naturally.

Spock underwent an earlier *Pon farr* on Stardate 3372.7 (2267), and had to return to Vulcan to take T'Pring as his wife, or he would die. And though they were betrothed to each other, telepathically bonded while children, T'Pring rejected Spock and chose Kirk to fight Spock. Knowing that regardless of the outcome, the man she preferred as her mate, Stonn, would still be hers.

"You humans have no conception," Spock explained to Kirk. "It strips our minds from us; it brings a . . . madness which rips away our veneer of civilization. It is the *Pon farr,* the time of mating.

"I had hoped I would be spared this, but the ancient drives are too strong. Eventually, they catch up with us . . . and we are driven by forces we cannot control to return home and take a wife. Or die."

T'Pring and Spock greeted each other with the traditional:

Parted from me and never parted; never and always touching and touched; we meet at the appointed place.

## Koon-ut-kal-if-fee

*Koon-ut-kal-if-fee,* meaning "marriage or challenge," reminds the Vulcans of the time before the Awakening, when they were required to kill to win their mates. This ancient practice is still in existence, as T'Pau explained, "What thee are about to see comes down from the time of the beginning, without change. This is the Vulcan heart. This is the Vulcan soul. This is our way. *Kah-if-farr!*"

T'Pring, though, responded "*Kal-if-fee!*" and issued a challenge on Spock's claim to her.

T'Pring chose her champion. "As it was in the dawn of our days, as it is today, as it will be for all tomorrows, I make my choice."

A ritual battle to the death begins with the *lirpa,* an ancient long-staffed weapon with a blade at one end and a bludgeon at the other. If both combatants survive, the battle would move on to *ahn-woon,* a single leather strap used as a whip or a noose. The victor may claim the female or set her free.

It is very clear to see that there is nothing logical about the *Pon farr.* It's a time when instinct and emotion dominate over reason. Anyone who has experienced it understands that it must simply be followed to its natural resolution. The resolution includes three options: taking a mate, the ritual combat, or intensive meditation.

But when it came down to the final stages of the *Pon farr,* when Vorik struggled to maintain his composure, he said to Tuvok, "Sir, I declare the *Koon-ut-kal-if-fee.*"

Tuvok explained to the other crew members. "The ritual challenge. He intends to fight to win his mate."

Tom Paris, who had witnessed these proceedings, quickly stepped forward to the challenge. But Torres stepped front and center herself. Tuvok explained, "She has the right to choose her own defender, even herself." And Tuvok wanted to let them fight. "It is logical. Both must resolve their *Pon farr* before it kills them. We cannot wait to hear from *Voyager.*

"The risk of injury seems preferable to the certainty of dying from a chemical imbalance." He turned to Chakotay.

"Commander, I see no alternative but to follow Vulcan tradition.

"*Karifarr,*" Tuvok said. "Begin."

# Death Rituals

## *Katra*

The belief in *katra* is the basics of Vulcan faith. The *katra,* or living spirit of a Vulcan, is what they believe lives on after death. The preservation of the *katra* happens right before death, when Vulcans can meld with another and pass their *katra* on.

"When I was younger," Tuvok explained, "I accepted it *(katra)* without question. In recent years, I have experienced doubts.

"I do believe there is more within each of us than science has yet explained."

After Spock's death (Stardate 8210.3), Sarek confronted Captain Kirk and demanded a mind-meld to find Spock's *katra.*

"You denied him his future," Sarek told Kirk, who didn't see much of a future for his deceased heroic friend.

"Only his body was in death, Kirk," Sarek explained. "And you were the last one to be with him; then you must know that you should have come with him to Vulcan."

"Why?"

"Because he asked you to, he entrusted you with his very essence, with everything that was not of the body. He asked you to bring him to us and to bring him that which he gave you, his *katra,* his living spirit."

"Sir, your son meant more to me than you could know. I would have given my life if it would have saved his. Believe me when I tell you, he made no request of me," Kirk sadly informed him.

"He would not have spoken of it openly," Sarek insisted. "Kirk, I must have your thoughts. May I join your mind?"

"Certainly,"

Sarek and Kirk sat, and the Ambassador placed his hand on Kirk's face. They mind-melded and Sarek discovered something. "Forgive me, it is not here. I assumed he had mind-melded with you; it is the Vulcan way when the body's end is near."

"We were separated; he couldn't touch me," Kirk revealed.

Sarek lamented, "Then everything that he was, everything that he knew, is lost."

"If there was that much at stake, Spock would have found a way!" Kirk insisted.

Kirk discovers that McCoy is the one Spock melded with; he had the Vulcan's *katra*.

## Fal-tor-pan

This specific Vulcan ritual of refusion, *fal-tor-pan*, was intended to reunite an individual's living spirit (or *katra)* to that person's body. Until 2285, the ritual had not been performed for centuries, but when Spock's body was regenerated at the Genesis Planet, Sarek requested the ritual, which proved successful.

For the first time in generations, a request was made for refusion. In a large Vulcan chamber on Mount Selaya, a gong was rung. Sarek led the procession, and Spock's body was placed on a ceremonial pedestal.

"*Kal to fala akal,*" T'Lar the Vulcan high priestess spoke. "Sarek, child of Skon, child of Solkar, the body of your son breathes still. What is your wish?"

"I ask for *fal-tor-pan,* the refusion," Sarek said.

"What you seek has not been done since ages past. And then only in legend. Your request is not logical," she stated.

"Forgive me, T'Lar," Sarek said, "my logic is uncertain where my son is concerned."

T'Lar continued the ritual, "Who is the keeper of the *katra?*"

The doctor stepped forward. "I am. McCoy, Leonard H., son of David."

"McCoy, son of David, since thou art human, we cannot expect thee to understand fully what Sarek has requested. Spock's body lives. With your approval, we shall use all our powers to return to his body that which you possess. But, McCoy, you must be warned; the danger to thyself is as grave as the danger to Spock. You must make the choice."

"I choose the danger. . . . A hell of a time to ask," he said in an aside to Kirk.

McCoy lay on a ceremonial pedestal slab like Spock. The priestess stood between them and recited, "*Been debow, navoon.*" The gong was rung. She turned to McCoy and placed her hand on his forehead. She placed her other hand on Spock and acted as the conduit for the meld. Lightning and thunder crashed. The assembled could only wait.

The gong was hit as Kirk stood by, watching. McCoy stepped down from the altar, noting, "I'm all right, Jim."

Kirk was glad, but he asked, "What about Spock?"

"Only time will answer that," Sarek said. "Kirk, I thank you."

"If I hadn't tried," Kirk admitted, "the cost would have been my soul."

At last, the hooded Spock walked down from the altar, surrounded by others. He hesitated and turned to Kirk and the rest of the crew. He looked them over, as if they were in an inspection. Then he faced Kirk. "My father says that you have been my friend. You came back for me. Why would you do this?"

"Because the needs of the one outweigh the needs of the many," Kirk replied, revising the quote from *A Tale of Two Cities* that Spock had cited.

The quote seemed to trigger a memory in Spock. "I have been and ever shall be your friend," he said, as naturally as if he hadn't just been reborn that day.

"Yes," Kirk smiled. "Yes, Spock."

"The ship is out of danger?"

"You saved the ship," Kirk told him. "You saved us all, don't you remember?"

"Jim," Spock recalled. "Your name is Jim."

"Yes," Kirk smiled.

The *fal-tor-pan* expresses the connection Vulcans have to their primitive past, to the time before logic became their focus, but it is this step into the past, the illogical, that completes them.

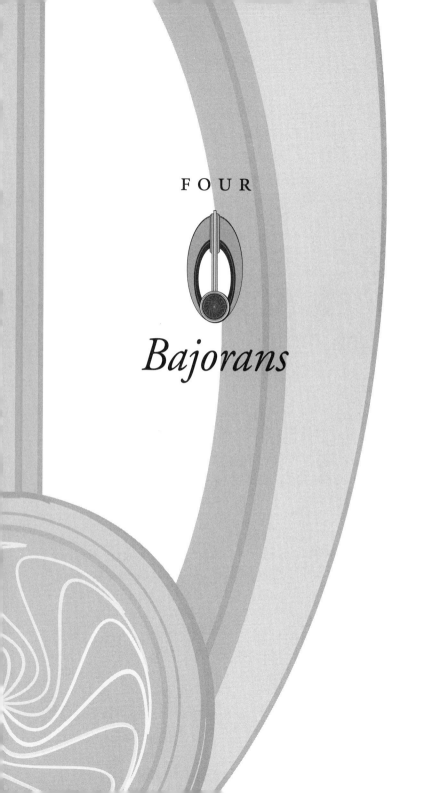

FOUR

*Bajorans*

Descendants of architects, artists, and philosophers, the Bajorans are a peaceful, spiritual people who were subject to Cardassian oppression for over forty years.

Many ancient customs have returned to favor following the ending of the Cardassian Occupation.

The *kai,* the supreme religious leader, is now openly elected by the Vedek Assembly. Bajor's political system embraces the tenets of the Prophets.

## Religion

The Bajoran wormhole is considered the home of the Celestial Prophets, and some religious leaders have fought to keep any scientific interpretation of this phenomena out of Bajoran teachings. Receiving safe passage through the wormhole is considered the work of the Prophets, rather than the result of skilled navigation.

The Nine Orbs, or Tears of the Prophets, are also a subject of much debate. Believed to be gifts from the Prophets to the Bajorans, they were ejected from the wormhole. Eight of the Orbs were stolen by Cardassia during the Occupation. The Orb of Prophecy and Change was the only one retained by the Bajorans during the Occupation, and it was well protected and highly regarded as a source of their personal strength. Other Orbs, since returned to Bajor, include the Orb of Time, which, when used properly, has the ability to transport someone back in time. The Orb of Wisdom provides the participant with new insight and clarity. The people turn to their Orbs for answers and explanations. Four Orbs removed by the Cardassians are still missing; many Bajorans consider this as a sign of the Prophets' displeasure while others dismiss it as the fortunes of war.

Bajoran's spiritual nature translates into their personal lives. Each stage of life is celebrated. Prayer such as

*Jia'kaja tre'nu'toli'a rem . . . La'por l'lana kos . . . l'nar tan'a'tali nor . . .*

which is said over a suffering person, comforts the speaker as much as the one being prayed over.

## Birth Ritual

The Bajoran Birth Ritual is a very specific and delicate procedure that fully welcomes the newborn into the world, Bajoran society, and the arms of the Prophets.

The traditional birthing room is decorated with pillows, wall tapestries, and a small shrine with burning incense.

The mother wears a garment that is a cross between a hospital gown and an ornate robe. She is seated on a table, inclined for back support, and made as comfortable as possible.

The Bajoran midwife stands at the foot of the table wearing traditional robes. The midwife has a *cabasa*. Two other participants hold a beaded gourd and a small gong. All three of these instruments are traditional noisemakers.

In solemn rhythmic succession, they play their devices, each making a series of specific noises. The mother practices a kind of controlled breathing exercise keyed to these sounds. It's up to each of the three to carry a consistent rhythm so she can enter a state of deep relaxation.

When the time comes, the new baby gets a traditional Bajoran greeting:

Awake, child. (To the twist of a *cabasa*.)
We await you with love. (The gourd is rattled.)
(The gong is tapped.) And welcome you into the world.

## Gratitude Festival

*Peldor joi!* That's the traditional greeting for the Bajoran Gratitude Festival, which is the biggest holiday of the year. Also known simply as the *Peldor* Festival, this annual celebration has the participants write their troubles on Renewal Scrolls and then burn those scrolls, symbolizing the turning to ashes of the problems. The temple chimes ring in celebration, and the smell of *bateret* leaves, burned as incense, fills the air.

During the third annual Gratitude Festival Celebration on Deep Space 9 when Major Kira Nerys presided over the ceremony, she intoned the ancient Bajoran blessing

*Tesra Peblor impatri bren. Bentel vetan ullon sten.*

A flask was tilted, slowly pouring a burning liquid into a metal brazier and setting its contents alight. Then Kira continued the blessing in Standard:

And now, I have the honor of placing the first
Renewal Scroll into the fire.
As the scrolls burn, may all our troubles turn to
ashes with them.

And as the scroll burns,

Now for the next twenty-six hours I expect you to
enjoy yourselves.

The whole point of the Gratitude Festival is that you should put your troubles behind you and make a fresh start. Captain Sisko even insisted the festivities take place during the Dominion War, because, as he explained, "War or no war, we have a lot to be grateful for. It's important to remember that."

# Rite of Separation

The Rite of Separation is an old Bajoran custom. When a couple decides that their relationship has come to an end, they spend several days celebrating their parting. It's a way to remember all the good times and to seek out new opportunities.

This particular rite has caused some non-Bajorans to comment that it's a wise and ancient custom.

With a witness, the participants kneel in front of each other, reciting the ceremony.

Our paths have grown apart,

the woman states, then drinks from a shallow bowl, and hands that to her companion, who says:

What was one is now two.

And, he sips from the bowl.

The time of sharing is over.

She takes the bowl from him and smashes it, saying,

May the Prophets guide you toward the path of happiness.

To which he replies:

And may they walk with you always.

The two lean in to each other in what looks to be a kiss, but before they touch, they ritualistically turn away.

# Weddings

Traditional Bajoran weddings are conducted in accordance with ancient texts. One of those texts, which has proven to be a favorite, is Horran's Seventh Prophecy, beginning:

> He will come to the palace carrying the chalice.
> Overflowing with sweet spring wine.

For Bajorans, the possibility of having the Emissary conduct their marriage ceremony is a great honor. Though called upon for many other duties as Emissary and captain, Sisko would take time to conduct this joyful task, and would speak in Bajoran.

> *Boray pree hadokee. Tolata impars boresh.*
> *Preeya Rom. Preeya Leeta, abrem vare atel.*

He was apt to conclude the service with an ancient Earth standard wedding conclusion:

> You may kiss the bride.

It is considered good luck for a Bajoran bride to wear a Navatar shawl, which is made of fine cloth, covered in an intricate pattern of vivid colors and embroidery. Kasidy Yates had one made in preparation for her wedding to Sisko. Though early reports stated that Sisko and Kasidy Yates were preparing for a small ceremony, the Bajorans expected a lavish affair as the Emissary warranted. The bride would need fifty-one girls for dais bearers, as just a beginning. They planned for a Vedek to perform the ceremony, but Kai Winn volunteered, as a symbol of status and importance. It was supposed to be the biggest wedding Bajor had ever seen. However, the elaborate ceremony was not held. Instead a simple service was conducted by Admiral Ross, who performed a standard Starfleet wedding in the wardroom of Deep Space 9.

# Death Rituals

## Death Chant

The funeral and death rituals of the Bajorans are very specific. The death chant itself is reputed to be over two hours long. In death, a person's life force, *pagh,* is considered much more important than the body. It is hoped that the *pagh* find passage to the Prophets and that the Prophets welcome the recently deceased into the next phase.

## Borhyas

Not quite the *pagh,* the *Borhyas* is the spirit or soul of a Bajoran. The difference is that a *Borhyas* is more like a ghost, the lost souls of ancient Earth stories. Bajorans are taught that as *Borhyas,* they need to make peace with their former lives, to say good-bye to the people they leave behind.

## Duranja

The *duranja,* the ceremonial lamp for the dead, is an ornate candleholder that is over a meter high. Its flame is kept continually lit to honor the recently deceased.

The prayer said over a *duranja* is:

Raka-ja ut shala morala . . . ema bo roo kana . . .
Uranak . . . ralanon Bareil . . . propeh va nara ehsuk
shala-kan vunek.

Or:

Do not let him walk alone . . . guide him on his journey. . . . Protect . . . the one named Bareil . . . take him
into the gates of heaven.

# Religious Celebrations

## Days of Atonement

The Days of Atonement are a high holy festival. Throughout Bajor, many make a trip to a monastery. The vedeks offer retreats where the faithful can meditate and pray. A typical prayer is:

Today we begin prayer and meditation in preparation
for the Days of Atonement.
    May the Prophets walk with us as we begin our
journey.

## Time of Cleansing

The Time of Cleansing is a monthlong ritual in which the partici-
pants abstain from worldly pleasures. Some observers have noted that a people who live as well and cleanly as the Bajorans would have few reasons for abstinence. Others point to the importance of their religion as an explanation for keeping this practice. Bajorans are admired and commended for their obser-

vation of such customs, though they do tend to rush for mugs of synthenol the first day of the new month.

## *Ha'mara*

Celebrating the arrival of the Emissary is the annual holiday called *Ha'mara*. The Bajorans fast to show the Prophets gratitude for sending the Emissary to them. On the eve of *Ha'mara*, there is a spectacular Festival of Lights in Bajor's capital.

Captain Sisko's discomfort at being designated the Emissary kept him away from the celebration, though he was always invited by the grateful Bajorans.

## The Emissary

In Bajoran religious history, the Emissary was foretold to be the one to find the Celestial Temple, free, and unite the Bajoran people. When a Starfleet officer, Benjamin Sisko, discovered the wormhole (2369) on the edge of the Alpha Quadrant, he was declared the Emissary.

Sisko was uncomfortable with this designation, but he respected the Bajorans' beliefs. His position as a religious figure was difficult for Starfleet to accept as well. There were a few recorded instances—and probably a few unknown—when a Starfleet officer attempted to pass himself off as a god or some figure in the society's mythology in order to extract information or gifts. But those situations were dealt with and were with pre-warp societies. Sisko's role as Emissary to the Bajoran people, however, aided them in rebuilding their world, allowing them to consider applying for admittance into the Federation.

While any Starfleet officer would be uncomfortable with this situation, Captain Sisko managed to cope. He came to accept that

the Bajorans on the station looked up to him for guidance and prayer. He could be asked for the occasional blessing over a young girl's *ih'tana* ceremony. He was called upon to bless newlyweds, praying:

> *Zhia'kaluh tar'eh any suur . . . te'von aka'lu rez . . .*
> *ka'voor, mat'ana kel.*

Every spring, on Deep Space 9, the Emissary held a ceremony to bless the women on the station who wanted to become mothers. Before his disappearance—the Bajorans believe he has joined the Prophets—Captain Sisko as the Emissary conducted the rite. After he married Kasidy Yates, she was looked to for the blessings. Bajorans give a traditional offering of *koganko* pudding signifying their desire for children.

## Arrival of Akorem and Sisko

Akorem Laan was a highly regarded poet of the twenty-second century. He disappeared only to return to Bajor two hundred years later. He emerged from the wormhole, the Celestial Temple, and claimed to be the Emissary since the Prophets had taken such interest in him.

Sisko graciously relinquished the role of Emissary—he once told Jadzia Dax, "It's just hard to get used to being a religious icon"—and Akorem began to implement radical changes in Bajoran society.

But Sisko regretted his decision when problems arose. Akorem's changes would push Bajor back to a time before the Occupation, when there was a strict caste system in place, the *D'jarra*. The system infringed on individual rights and forced people into positions they were no longer suited for. This new system

would have forced Bajor to withdraw from Federation consideration, since societies with caste systems are not accepted.

According to one of the spiritual leaders, Vedak Porta, "You must do what the Emissary has asked and follow your *D'jarra* with all your heart. Because if you give yourself over to the Prophets, they will guide you along the path they've chosen for you. And you'll have more joy than you ever thought possible."

Bajoran society seemed headed for conflict. Fortunately, according to Kira Nerys, the Prophets intervened and marked Sisko as their true Emissary. They then used their mysterious powers to send Akorem back home to his time.

## Pagh'tem'far

Sisko's close connection with the Prophets of the Celestial Temple occasionally expressed itself in the form of sacred visions, called *pagh'tem'far*.

One particular *pagh'tem'far* could have led to Sisko's death, but as many Bajorans believe, there is nothing the Prophets do without a reason. Guided by his vision, Sisko eventually found the lost Bajoran city of B'hala. Another *pagh'tem'far* led him to the planet Tyree, where he found the Orb of the Emissary. The opening of this Orb led to the reopening of the wormhole, returning the Prophets to the Celestial Temple, and banished the Pah-wraiths.

Kai Winn, who opposed Sisko on many occasions, did pray for him during the time of the B'hala mission:

He asks for your guidance. Let him see with your eyes.
Lift the veil of darkness that obscures his path.

Another *pagh'tem'far* led to Sisko's recommendation that Bajor not accept admittance into the Federation, angering Starfleet command. But that vision saved many lives after the start of the Dominion War, as did Bajor's signing a nonaggression pact with the Dominion at Sisko's urging.

## The Reckoning and Kosst Amojan

In Shabren's Fifth Prophecy, the ancient text tells of the Evil One being destroyed, bringing about a thousand years of peace, leading to a Golden Age on a reborn Bajor.

Leading to this Golden Age is the Reckoning, the battle

between the Prophets and Pah-wraiths. An ancient tablet was discovered to read:

Welcome, Emissary

The time of Reckoning is at hand. The Prophets will weep, and their sorrow will consume the Gateway to the Temple.

The Gateway was assumed to be Deep Space 9.
The translation progressed:

During the Reckoning, Bajorans are going to suffer horribly. Once the Reckoning begins, the Emissary will—

Unfortunately, the inscription at this point was damaged.

A Prophet took over Kira Nerys's body and offered up some information to Sisko when he asked what the Reckoning was.

"The end . . . or the beginning," the Prophet told Sisko.

"I don't understand," he said.

"I await Kosst Amojan" was the explanation.

Kai Winn knew the name. "The Evil One—a Pah-wraith banished from the Celestial Temple."

"You're saying a Pah-wraith will take corporeal form as well?" Sisko asked.

The kai cited the Fifth Prophecy as evidence of this foretold battle.

With a group of the Bajorans, Kai Winn prayed for the Prophets' victory over the Evil One. "*Tera dak ihsehlm ran embah.*" And the faithful replied, "*de-ram ta-meen.*"

The Reckoning did not commence as prophesized, due to the interference of Kai Winn. The Prophets were prepared for the destruction of the Evil One, but Winn was not. The Golden Age was halted.

## Capture of the Pah-wraiths

Many Bajorans believe that following the surrender of the Dominion in 2375, Benjamin Sisko traveled to the fire caves on Bajor, where he was finally able to trap the Pah-wraiths within the caves. With his final act, the Emissary ensured the survival of the Prophets and the Bajoran people. The Bajorans believe that Sisko is no longer in our plane of existence, but is now one of the Prophets.

# FIVE

*Ferengi*

Ferengi society has been undergoing change on a scale that many Federation observers once thought impossible. In 2374, there was an amendment to the Bill of Opportunities. Once adopted, this amendment made it legal for females to wear clothes. This one sweeping change would have been enough for any other nagus, but Grand Nagus Zek took steps to pass several social programs—wage subsidies, retirement benefits, health care, to name a few—all funded by a progressive income tax. His final act as grand nagus was to ensure his legacy with the appointment of Rom as his successor. As with any radical change, there are naysayers who bemoan the changes and lament the end of an era, but as a whole, Ferengi society has embraced the changes, seeing them as new ways to promote profit. That one core idea—the creation of profit—is the driving force of the Ferengi. Of course, everyone knows about the Rules of Acquisition, but outsiders don't need to know them all, as every Ferengi does; they need only understand that at the heart of this society and these people is profit.

## Naming Day

Naming Day is a coming-of-age ritual practiced by the Ferengi. A boy's parents give him presents. Within the family—which has given the most information on Ferengi culture—Quark substituted old vegetables for Rom's presents. He then sold the presents at a higher price than their father had paid for them. In Ferengi culture, Quark made his father proud with this act, and at such a young age, too.

## Attainment Ceremony

The Attainment Ceremony, while largely considered a formality, is one of the most stressful events in a young Ferengi's life, as well as the most important. Ferengi are forced to choose between their best friend and a bar of latinum, and no Ferengi is recorded as having chosen the friend. With recent changes, females have been integrated into active society, but there is no present record of an Attainment Ceremony for a female.

Done properly, the ceremony is held in a well-lit room, with both the latinum and the friend equidistant from the child. The bar of latinum should be as shiny as possible to allow for the boy to see it well. It is suggested that the friend be strapped down as not to distract the participant. There is a Southern Ferenginar version of this ritual that isn't suggested, due to the high possibility of injury: both boys fight each other over the bar of latinum, and this could affect the long-term investment growth of the outcome. The Attainment Ceremony reflects the 21st Rule of Acquisition: "Never place friendship above profit."

After successful completion of one's Attainment Ceremony, Ferengi Bylaw, Section 105, Subparagraph 10, states, "Upon reaching adulthood, Ferengi males must purchase an apprenticeship from a suitable role model." Lieutenant Nog chose Captain Benjamin Sisko. Nog's perseverance in pursuit of his goal proved to Sisko that he would be an asset to Starfleet, and his "apprenticeship" began.

## Welcoming Ceremony

The Welcoming Ceremony is a basic ritual upon entering a Ferengi home. The owner of the house recites:

> Welcome to our home. Please place your imprint on the legal waivers and deposit your admission fee in the basket by the door. Remember, my house is my house.

To which the guest answers:

As are its contents.

The guest then gives back the towel he used to wipe off the constant Ferenginar rain.

# Weddings

## Ferengi Love

The recent major changes in Ferengi culture open up a whole new universe for the Ferengi. Before this, though, Ferengi entered into marriage with little or no thought of the female. Ferengi are known to have more than a passing interest in non-Ferengi women; the present grand nagus has a Bajoran wife.

Change was in the air prior to Grand Nagus Rom's ascension, with the former grand nagus, Zek, allowing his love interest, Ishka (who happens to be mother to Quark and Rom) equal footing in all things; she was also a financial advisor. One of their more romantic exchanges is reproduced here:

Zek: "My dear, you reek of tube grubs."

Ishka: "So do you, lobekins."

Zek: "Are your ears tingling?"

She nods.

Zek: "Mine too."

Quark's traditional—or old-fashioned, as some may suggest—reaction to his mother's and brother's actions is one of simple disgust, because according to the 94th Rule of Acquisition, "Females and finances don't mix."

## Waiver of Property and Profit

The Waiver of Property and Profit (WP&P) is a now antiquated form that forced the bride-to-be to sign over all rights to the husband's estate, due to the old law that Ferengi females aren't allowed to own property or profit. In the event of the end of the marriage, the wife would have no claim on anything. In fact, the 139th Rule of Acquisition states: "Wives serve, brothers inherit."

Rom, leading the way for the new Ferenginar, gave up the WP&P for his Bajoran wife, Leeta. He also gave his entire fortune over to the Bajoran War Orphans fund, letting her salary be all they needed prior to his ascension to grand nagus.

Prior to the Ferengi Bill of Opportunities ammendment in 2374, when the right for females to wear clothes was recognized, the bride was naked at a Ferengi wedding. Unlike Betazoid weddings where it is encouraged that everyone be naked, the Ferengi custom was to keep all females unclothed even following the wedding.

The bridal auction and latinum dance are other traditions of Ferengi weddings. While no Ferengi now will explain what these are, it can be deduced that both the bridal auction and latinum dance were ways for the groom to profit from his wedding. An ancient human wedding custom had wedding guests give the bride and groom an amount of money to allow the guest to dance with the bride. This money was added to the shared gifts of the newlyweds. While there is no sharing, the latinum dance could be a parallel development. Since females weren't allowed to own anything, the bridal auction wasn't the bride auctioning off her property to guests, but her father could be required to have an auction to pay for the wedding.

Quark has been quoted as saying, "All I know is that any marriage where the female's allowed to speak and wear clothing is doomed to failure."

## Death Rituals

A fitting way to honor the memory of great Ferengi entrepreneurs in death is the sale of the desiccated remains of the corpse. The body of the deceased is chopped into fifty-two disks, which are auctioned to the highest bidder on the Ferengi Futures Exchange or sold in person. Making a profit, even in death, encourages entry into the Divine Treasure. It is not uncommon—and encouraged—to charge admission to the eulogy.

After planning to split himself up into fifty-two disks and having begun the bidding, Quark—who thought he was dying—said: "My death is nothing to get upset about; I'm making money on it."

Following death and initial sales, pieces of more famous members of Ferengi society go out for resale as valuable souvenirs. While reselling pieces of Plegg, Quark's sales pitch on Plegg went as follows: "What Ferengi could resist the honor of owning a small piece of the man who took a computer chip and turned it into the modular holosuite industry . . . a small piece of the man who brought holographic entertainment to the most remote parts of this quadrant, creating profit centers from societies that could barely afford to feed their own people."

Quark was asking only three strips of latinum, a fair price for a Ferengi hero, with a Ferengi Seal of Dismemberment proving authenticity. Unfortunately for him, Plegg was alive.

Death without dismemberment profit was not looked upon highly in Ferengi society.

## Divine Treasury

In death, Ferengi are still expected to turn a profit. Ferengi mythology says that financially successful Ferengi go to the Divine Treasury after death. There, the Registrar awaits them at the entrance, and if the new arrival is worthy to enter, the Registrar will accept a bribe and usher him inside.

The Divine Treasury is said to shine with the glow of pure latinum. Over ornate double doors hangs a sign: "Please have your profit-and-loss statements ready for inspection before entering the Divine Treasury." This is where the Blessed Exchequer is, the mystical accountant who presides over the Treasury.

Within the Divine Treasury is the Celestial Auction, where Ferengi bid on a new life, returning to Ferenginar to profit anew.

The changes in Ferengi society, however, have people believing less of the tradition behind the Treasury. Over 40 percent of the population no longer believes that you have to buy your way into the Divine Treasury when you die.

## Vault of Eternal Destitution

Ferengi aim to profit for many reasons, the main one being the 18th Rule of Acquisition: "A Ferengi without profit is no Ferengi at all." But Ferengi who did not earn a profit in their mortal lives are thought to be doomed to the Vault of Eternal Destitution. No Ferengi would discuss it because of the fear of this failure. It's not known if the belief in the Divine Treasury is compatible with the belief in the Vault of Eternal Destitution.

## Great Material Continuum

Ferengi mythology says that the worlds in the universe are filled with too much of one thing and not enough of the other. Ferengi believe the Great Material Continuum flows through all the worlds like a river bringing the Ferengi back and forth between "have" and "want." If one can navigate this river successfully, one can be filled with all one desires.

Lieutenant Nog has great faith in the Great River, having learned about it as child, when he was still "a young lobling." Though the River can be treacherous, having faith that "the River will provide" did get Nog through a few "turns in the River" that benefited his Starfleet superiors.

## Ascension of the Grand Nagus

As Grand Nagus Zek grew older and saw that Ferenginar had to change, he saw fit to appoint a new kind of nagus. Rom's ascension to grand nagus was the precursor to the present adjustments in Ferengi society.

Zek informed Rom, "It's a great responsibility to stand at the bow of the Ferengi ship of state . . . a nagus has to navigate the waters of the Great Material Continuum. Avoid the shoals of bankruptcy and seek the strong winds of prosperity."

Profit is still the goal of the nagus, but now it's not the blind acquisition that had ruled Ferenginar.

# SIX

# Other Life-Forms, Cultures, and Experiences

Much like ancient Earth, the United Federation of Planets, their allies, and the non-allied worlds provide a great tapestry of cultures to explore. Some have offered up their traditions in full, and some have integrated them with others. Still others have held on to their rituals, keeping them hidden from outsiders and unknown to the Federation.

## Vision Quest

A custom of ancient Earth Native Americans, a vision quest helps people reexamine their lives. It allows for introspection, and though traditionally it was participated in during adolescence, it is not unheard of for adults to turn to the aid of a vision quest to get them through a particularly rough personal time.

*Voyager*'s first officer, Chakotay, is of Native American descent and participated in his own vision quests. He has also offered to be the guide for fellow crew members, including Captain Kathryn Janeway.

"*A-koo-chee-moya* . . . we are far from the sacred places of our grandfathers. We are far from the bones of our people. But perhaps there is one powerful being who will embrace this woman and give her the answers she seeks.

"Allow your eyes to close. Breathe to fuel the light in your belly, and let it expand, until the light is everywhere.

"Prepare yourself to leave this room, and this ship, and return to place where you were the most content and peaceful you have ever been. You can see all around you and hear the sounds of this place.

"You must not discuss with me what you see or you will offend your animal guide.

"As you continue to look around, you will become aware of

other life that shares this place with you. It will be the first animal you see that is the one you will speak to."

In a vision quest, oftentimes, subjects search for their animal guide to help find their inner strength. B'Elanna Torres, *Voyager's* chief engineer, is the only person known to have tried to kill an animal guide.

Wesley Crusher, while visiting Dorvan V, met with some of the transplanted Native American colonists and found himself introduced to his own vision quest within a *habak*. His quest led him to a personal realization.

The *habak* is a ceremonial chamber of great importance to the Native Americans. On Doran V it was located in a high tower; the only way in was by a ladder leading from a hole in the floor. The room itself was rectangular. Sunlight poured through a hole in the ceiling. There was a fire pit in the center of the room, and there was a ledge to sit on running along the wall.

The walls were decorated with colorful sacred wall hangings. Many elements of the twenty-fourth century were alongside elements representing reverence for their ancient ways. Another ledge had several dolls on it, dolls representing different spirits.

"Our culture is rooted in the past, but it is not limited to the past. The spirits of Klingons, Vulcans, Ferengi come to us just as the bear, the coyote, the parrot. There is no difference."

While waiting for something to occur, Crusher was straining to stay awake; he was sweating, he was exhausted. His eyes opened wide to reveal that Lakanta, his native host, was gone, but he heard a voice in the distance.

The smoke in the *habak* suddenly dissipated and Crusher found himself standing in the village that appeared like a dream place. The voice cried out again, and Crusher saw his father.

"You've reached the end, Wesley. You set out on a journey that wasn't your own. Now it's time to find the path that is truly yours. Don't follow me any further."

Crusher knew what his father was speaking to him about and tried to explain it to his mother. "I was participating in an Indian ritual; I had a vision. And in it," he paused, "Dad came to me. He told me not to follow him, that I had to find my own path."

It was this incident that moved Wesley Crusher to leave Starfleet Academy.

Chakotay had some advice for those he walked through vision quests, "You've only lived with the visions for a couple of days; that's not enough time to draw any conclusions. You've got to reflect on the images, examine them, allow them to stay alive in your mind.

"A vision quest isn't just a dream you dismiss after your first cup of coffee."

## ROMULANS

Life is difficult in the Romulan Star Empire, where everyone pretty much looks out for himself, but the Romulans are trying to put things back together. During the Dominion War, an uneasy alliance was formed between the Federation and the Romulans, who for a century used the Neutral Zone as their line in the sand. A tenuous alliance during that war between the Romulans and the Klingons was also established during that period. The combined forces of the Federation, the Klingon Empire, and the Romulan Empire led to the end of the war.

Romulans as a people are strong-willed warriors. They are capable of great compassion, but their aggressive nature is what the Federation has primarily experienced.

An offshoot of the Vulcan race, the Romulans founded their own Star Empire after their Vulcans brothers eschewed their emotional, violent tendencies for pure logic. Ambassador Spock has said, "The union of the Romulan and Vulcan people will not be achieved by politics. Or by diplomacy. But it will be achieved. The answer has been here in front of us all the time. And inexorable evolution toward a Vulcan philosophy has already begun: like the first Vulcans, these people are struggling to find a new enlightenment. It may take decades, centuries, for them to reach it, but they will, and I must help."

Romulans are quite honorable, and they hold honor in high regard, allowing even prisoners and enemies rights accorded to the average Romulan.

A Romulan commander told the crew of the *U.S.S. Enterprise,* NCC-1701 (Stardate 5027.3, 2268), "Execution of state criminals is both painful and unpleasant. I believe the details are unnecessary. The sentence will be carried out immediately after the charges have been recorded."

Spock spoke up, "I demand the Right of Statement, first."

"You understand Romulan tradition well," the commander said. "The right is granted."

"Thank you. I shall not require much time. No more than twenty minutes, I should say," Spock informed them.

"It should take less time than that to find your ally who stole the cloaking device. You will not die alone," the commander informed him. "Recording. The Romulan Right of Statement. Proceed, Commander Spock."

"My crime is sabotage. I freely admit my guilt. The oath I swore as Starfleet officer is both specific and binding. As long as I wear the uniform, it is my duty to protect the security of the

Federation. Clearly, your new cloaking device is a threat to that security. I carried out my duty."

"Everyone carries out his duty," the Romulan commander interrupted. "You state the obvious, Spock."

"There is no regulation regarding the content of my statement. May I continue?"

"Very well," the commander said, "Your twenty minutes are almost up."

As the *Enterprise* attempted to lock the transporter on Spock, in order to rescue him, he continued to buy them time.

" . . . Beyond the historic tradition of Vulcan loyalty . . . there is also the combined Romulan/Vulcan history of obedience of duty . . ." and they beamed Spock up.

The possibility of peace with the Romulans does exist, and it is only through combined efforts and continual education and understanding that this will be achieved in full.

# CARDASSIANS

A race that has known mostly war for the last few centuries, after a lifetime of peace and spirituality, the Cardassians survived on their resource-poor planet by becoming more aggressive with other life-forms. They do, though, place a high value on family.

During the Dominion War, public sentiment turned against their allegiance with the Dominion. The forces of the Dominion were then unleashed against the Cardassian people. The devastating loss of life at war's end was tallied at over one-point-five billion killed. Relief efforts have been pouring in from all over the Federation. Even the Bajoran government has provided aid to their one-time oppressors.

## Death Rituals

Colonel Kira Nerys faced the death of a Cardassian who came to see her as a daughter. Legate Ghemor asked her to his side. "Nerys, I know more about the Cardassian government than anyone else. Names, alliances, plots, things that could do a lot of good, in the right hands.

"There's a Cardassian tradition called *shri-tal*." Ghemor was energized by what he was going to suggest. "The dying give their secrets to their family, to use against their enemies. But I have no one left to carry my secrets. No one but you."

"Me?"

"Be my daughter one last time, Nerys," he requested. "Hear what I know, and use it as you see fit."

## Burial of the Dead

During a mission to find an old friend who was on a Cardassian ship that went missing, Kira was ordered to travel with Gul Dukat, who wanted to find the same ship.

The wreckage of the ship was found, and alongside the crash site, graves were found. Dukat went to them to find out who they were. He stopped Kira from helping him in the exhumation. "No. Our funeral rites are very strict. It would dishonor the dead if a non-Cardassian were to view the remains."

# TRILLS

One of the more unique life-forms in the galaxy are those known as Trills. Living a symbiotic, almost parasitic, existence, some Trills carry within them a wormlike creature, known as a symbiont, which passes on the knowledge that each successive host gains. Nearly half the Trill population is able to host a symbiont, but only a select few are up to the challenge, so rigorous testing and training procedures are conducted before a Trill can be joined.

Jadzia, who was a host to the Dax symbiont, told one initiate trainee, "The symbiont's influence is very strong, but you're the host. *You've* got to be strong enough to balance that influence with your own instincts.

"My job is to show you [*sic*] what it's like to function as a joined Trill. And that's all."

Traditionally, when the time comes and the current host is near death, the future host and current host are laid out on

tables side by side. The dripping wet wormlike symbiont is removed from the host, guided by a pair of hands out of the abdominal orifice. The symbiont is lifted, and ritual gold surgical scissors are used to sever the connection to the former host. The symbiont is placed on the abdomen of the new host and it burrows in. The new host is immediately filled with an enlightenment, and not only the memories of the symbiont but of all the prior hosts.

## Reassociation

The act of reassociation has very specific guidelines in Trill society. Reassociation occurs when a rejoined Trill meets someone who had been a part of a previous host's life. It's "against the rules" to have a close relationship with someone from an earlier Trill's existence.

"It's more of a taboo, really," Dr. Bashir conceded. "Having a relationship with a lover from a past life is called 'reassociation,' and the Trill feel very strongly that it's . . . unnatural.

"The whole point of joining is to allow the symbiont to accumulate experiences over the span of many lifetimes. But in order to move from host to host, the symbiont has to let go of the past, let go of parents, children, siblings, even spouses."

Kira insisted, "There must be *some* Trill that 'reassociate' with people from their past."

"I asked Dax the same question," Bashir confirmed, "and it seems there have been a few cases . . ."

"And what happened?"

"They were exiled from the Trill homeworld," Bashir informed her.

"That would mean their symbionts would never be joined to new hosts," Kira realized.

"Exactly," Bashir said. "When the hosts die, the symbionts would die with them.

". . . To a joined Trill, nothing is more important than protecting the life of the symbiont. Nothing."

## Zhian'tara

A joined Trill is required to meet previous hosts of the symbiont through Zhian'tara, the Rite of Closure. This is performed by non-joined Trills; usually friends of the current host act as a conduit for the previous host and the life force to inhabit their bodies. Jadzia Dax asked Odo, Bashir, Sisko, Kira, Quark, O'Brien, and Leeta to be her hosts for the Zhian'tara.

The guardian, an unjoined Trill whose sole purpose is to care for symbionts, telepathically transfers the memories of the former host into the temporary host's body as the ritual begins.

The Trill guardian arrived on DS9 and prepared a triangular altar. The altar had a reflective, almost mirrorlike surface. A small cauldron of whitish liquid bubbled over a flame in the center of the altar.

The guardian was standing behind Dax and Kira, who was first up to accept the prior host's memories. Their eyes were closed; they looked meditative.

Speaking in the ancient Trill language, sounding like a Gregorian chant, the guardian said,

I'nora, ja'kala Dax. Zhian'shee, Lela tanus rem, Gon'dar, Jadzia tor . . .

The guardian placed a hand on the small of Dax's back and to the back of Kira's head.

*Jadzia, zhian'tara volc, Tu Dax, zhian'tani ress, Zhiar'par, Lela Guru'koj . . .*

There is no direct translation of the chant, though it may be more of a relaxation technique, a mantra to allow for the memories to move from one calm body to another calm body.

An energy discharge emanated from Dax's belly, and in a

quick flash, snaked across the guardian's body into Kira's head. Her body seemed to deflate; she stopped breathing.

When the guardian took his hands off the women, Kira took a sharp breath, and her body filled with life. The glint in her eye was somehow different than usual.

Dax and she regarded each other for a long time.

"Kira?" Dax approached.

Kira broke into a smile, and when she spoke, even the timbre of her voice was different. "No," she corrected. "Lela."

Following the transference, the guardian asked some questions and confirmed that the memories had moved. The answers to questions she could have answered earlier were missing from Dax's mind, but the temporary host of Lela knew the answers.

# DRAYANS

Drayans, natives of the Delta Quadrant, traditionally avoid contact with outsiders. Meeting with the *Starship Voyager* was an anomaly. However, the *Voyager* crew was warmly greeted with a traditional blessing:

> May this day find you at peace and leave you with hope.

## Death Ritual

Drayan First Prelate Alcia asked the crew to leave their zone of space. But on a moon, Crysata—sacred to the Drayans—Tuvok discovered a different side to the Drayans. Lost Drayan children told him that the adults he saw didn't want to bring the children back. This was the final ritual, when the *morrok* came to take them away.

"The Scrolls say we should be happy . . . that when we die, the energy inside us is set free," Tressa, one of the children, explained.

But Corin didn't believe it. "Is it true? Is that what really happens?"

"There's no reason to fear for anyone's safety on the Crysata. It's a blessed haven, sheltered and unspoiled. Which is the very reason I can't allow you to go there under any circumstances." The prelate told Captain Janeway why she could not search for Tuvok's downed shuttle. Compromise was finally reached, and Alcia, the first prelate, accompanied Janeway to the moon.

The children remained scared and unwilling to go, but Alcia comforted them. "It's perfectly natural to be frightened. You're taking a step into the unknown. The Attendants would have helped you prepare yourselves. You were never meant to face this time alone."

"At this age," she explained, "they become easily confused. Their memories are clouded.

"Near the end of life, we reach a stage of complete innocence. We free ourselves from all responsibility to this life. Then we leave it peacefully.

"This is a normal biological process, which begins the day we are created. The energy contained within our bodies remains cohesive for a limited number of years, and then it's released. Nothing can change that."

This moon, and specifically the cave they were at, was sacred to the Drayans.

"We believe this is where the very first spark of life was created. We are all compelled by a powerful instinct to return here at the end, to complete the cycle, and rejoin the infinite energy."

Alcia turned to Tressa, who was in fact quite old despite her outward appearance. "Do you feel it calling to you?" She held her hand out to the "girl," who shrank back, calling to Tuvok.

"She can offer you better guidance than I," he told Tressa.

"You said you would protect me," she cried.

"I cannot protect you from the natural conclusion of life . . . nor would I try," he responded. "Vulcans consider death to be the completion of a journey. There is nothing to fear."

"I won't be afraid," confirmed Tressa. "Not if you're with me."

Alcia approached Tressa, wishing, "May this night see you safely home.

"Attending a child on the Crysata is an honorable role," she said to Tuvok. "You've fulfilled it well.

"The final moment of life is the most sacred, most private time," Alcia said to Janeway.

"I hope you can accept my sincere apologies for disturbing your traditions," the captain offered.

## TALARIANS

Talarian tradition came into conflict with more than Starfleet regulations when a long-lost child turned up on a Talarian ship—he was the grandson of a Starfleet admiral.

The human boy was raised by the Talarians and believed himself to be one of them. When the boy was returned to the *U.S.S. Enterprise* NCC-1701-D (Stardate 44143.7, 2367), the crew discovered that Jono was Jeremiah Rossa. But this once human child had embraced the traditions of the Talarians. Jono made "the *B'Nar*—the mourning—until I am back with my brothers." The *B'Nar* consists of

a rhythmic high-pitched shriek that can go on for hours. "It is the custom of my people when they are in distress," explained Jono.

The Talarian captain, Endar, explained the tradition of taking the son of a slain enemy to replace the son he lost to the same enemy. He claimed the human boy as his son and family.

Jono was old enough, according to Talarian tradition, to make his own decision of staying with his Talarian father or going back to his human family. Troi suggested that Jono might choose to stay with the humans, and Riker tried to anticipate whether Endar would abide by that decision. "If Endar respects Talarian customs," Data noted, "he may have to. According to their tradition, a male child of fourteen had reached the age of decision. They had undergone a ceremony of initiation and after that have the freedom to make their own choice."

The boy chose the only family he ever knew and returned to the Talarians.

## KRIOS and VALT MINOR

According to the records of Captain Picard, on Stardate 47761.3, "In an effort to bring an end to their centuries-long war, Krios and Valt Minor have agreed to a Ceremony of Reconciliation, to be held aboard the *Enterprise* at a point midway between their two systems."

The Kriosian ambassador, Briam, was astonished at the holodeck's version of the ancient Temple of Akada, an opulent, golden ceremonial temple where the ceremony would take place. "It is this temple that bonds Krios and Valt, gentlemen," he told Picard and La Forge. "Two brothers once ruled a vast empire from this site, until they were torn apart by their love for an extraordinary woman. This is where the wars began. And this is where they shall end."

The Kriosian gift—a beautiful woman named Kamala—was freed from her ceremonial container early due to Ferengi interference. She explained her metamorphic empathy, proclaiming herself, "A mutant. A biological curiosity, if you will. With the ability to sense what a potential mate wants, what he needs, what gives him the greatest pleasure, and then to become that for him."

Riker, naturally, reacted to this. "You mean, you change according to whatever man you're with?"

"Until I reach the stage of bonding," she told him, "when I must imprint myself the requirements of one man, to serve as his perfect partner in life."

The Ceremony of Reconciliation required assistance from Picard, who had to play a percussion instrument. He used a small hammer to strike the chimes seven times. There was a strict cadence. He also had to read from the ancient scroll, in the proper language.

The man to whom Kamala was betrothed, Alrik, was more interested in the treaty and trade agreements than in the beautiful woman who waited for him. During the journey Kamala had bonded with Picard, but her sense of duty was what she heeded when she said her simple ceremonial line, "I am for you, Alrik of Valt."

# MERIDIANS

For a people who live their physical lives in brief moments, waiting to be freed from their dimensional hibernation, each and every action is savored. Nothing is more savored than the first meal the inhabitants of Meridian have together following each awakening.

## First Meal

It seemed like a planet out of nowhere, but Seltin Rakal of Meridian explained to Sisko, "Not nowhere, Commander—it came from a dimension that intersects with this one.

"I could explain it in greater detail, if you're interested. We were just about to sit down for First Meal—why don't you join us?"

A feast was set forth in the Meridian village commons. "It's good to be together again around this table after so long," Seltin toasted. "What's more, we're fortunate to have visitors to share First Meal with us."

There were nods and murmurs of agreement and then everyone began eating. The people of Meridian eat slowly, with great relish, deliberately, savoring every moment.

Seltin explained to the DS9 crew that when they are in the other dimension, the people of Meridian are noncorporeal, and it's like no time has passed when they slip back into the corporeal dimension. After sixty years, fellow Meridian Deral noted, "We always look forward to this existence . . . and its many pleasures."

# Q CONTINUUM

One could deduce that Q's dealings with humanoid life-forms have become a bit of a ritual . . . and a bit of a holiday on occasion. Much like the ancient Greek and Roman gods, who were well known to come down to Earth to play with the humans, to see how they would react, how they worshipped, or even adapted to change, Q brings himself down to a human level . . . and finds humanity bemusing. But he does approach the concepts of humanity . . . in his own way.

Q's reported run-ins with the crews of the *Enterprise,* Deep Space 9, and *Voyager* have provided humanity with some insight into this immortal tribe of watchers. The Q, who seems to have a particular fascination for Captain Jean-Luc Picard, was an anomaly. As Guinan, an El-Aurian member of the *Enterprise* crew, noted, "Not all of the Q are like this one. Some are almost respectable."

And when he needed to explain the Continuum to Commander Will Riker, Q said, "The limitless dimensions of the galaxy in which we exist, we could hardly be capable of acting in ways that seem to be astonishing to you, if we were limited to the primitive dimensions in which you live, dimensions which would make us prisoners of time and space."

Though limitless, the Q Continuum was subject to its own problems and suffered a war of wills. A single Q, who took the human name Quinn, killed himself—with Q's assistance—igniting a battle for individual thought.

But getting to that point took years of interaction, because of what Q is (what they are). "To put it simply, we are omnipotent. There is nothing—nothing—we can't do."

And as much as Q interacts with humans, messes with them, there are still things that get to him. "These mating rituals you humans indulge in really are quite disgusting." As everyone knows, the more you discuss your dislike for something, the more likely it is that you are jealous that you don't have it.

"This human emotion of love is a dangerous thing, Picard. You are obviously ill equipped to handle it. She's found a vulnerability in you," Q said of Vash, "a vulnerability that I've wanted to find for years. If I had known this sooner, I would have arrived as a female. Mark my words, Jean-Luc, this is your Achilles heel."

The Q Continuum, it has been reported, made it a regular habit to watch other life-forms interact, to philosophize on their actions, and to interfere only when they thought it necessary, or—in Q's case—when they felt like it.

# OCAMPA

A calm, soothing people, the Ocampa suffered greatly at the hands of explorers who accidentally devastated the environment of their planet in the Delta Quadrant. The explorers stayed with them, taking responsibility for their actions, helping the Ocampa survive in an underground city, protecting them. Ocampa can speak to each other verbally and telepathically, and there are hints of latent psychokinetic powers.

Their life cycle only allows them nine years of life, but a full life in human terms is experienced.

## *Elogium*

*Elogium* is the time of change. As Kes explained, it is "when our bodies prepare for fertilization."

Janeway likened it to the human equivalent, puberty. But Kes, at two, is too young for this to happen to her. Unfortunately, as she explained, "The *elogium* occurs only once. If I'm ever going to have a child—it has to be *now.*"

## *Rolisisin*

Once the plans were set—Kes and Neelix decided to be parents—it was time to begin specific rituals. "Before we begin the mating process, I have to go through a—certain ritual," Kes told Neelix. "The *rolisisin . . .*"

"What does *that* involve?"

"One of my parents has to massage my feet until my tongue begins to swell."

Neelix asked, "Where do you plan to find a parent?"

She decided to ask the Doctor, but Neelix became jealous despite Kes's protestation that, "It's a ritual; someone has to do it."

While the ritual was being performed, Kes explained its significance to the Doctor. "If I were home now, my father would be performing the *rolisisin* with me. It's a time for parent and child to move into a new kind of relationship. As the child has her own child, the parent must acknowledge her true adulthood."

## Death Rituals

*Morilogium* is the final phase of the Ocampan life span, usually occurring around age nine. Kes expressed the beliefs of her people about death before she left *Voyager*. Bodies are buried beneath the soil, and it is thought that their *comra*—soul, spirit, the essence of their being—is released into the afterlife. Kes experienced something like this without actually dying when she was transformed into a noncorporeal being of pure energy.

# KAELONS

## Death Rituals

The Resolution, to Kaelons, was the perfect idea: to ease the pain of watching loved ones whither away, the age of sixty became the ritual year to end one's life. It was considered more dignified and preferable to ending up in "death-watch facilities."

Because they were isolationists, little was known about the people of Kaelon II, until Stardate 44805.3 (2367), when they had an encounter with the *Starship Enterprise*.

The time of the Resolution brings forth family and friends, and the person who is ending his life is wined, dined, and honored for his achievements and then expected to kill himself.

Ambassador Lwaxana Troi, then traveling aboard the *Enterprise*, considered it barbaric and told the scientist Timicin so.

Timicin defended his people's actions. "Until fifteen or twenty centuries ago, we had no 'Resolution,' no such concern for our elders. As people aged, their health failed; they became invalids. Those who could no longer be cared for by their families were put away in death-watch facilities, where they simply waited in loneliness for the end to come, often for years.

"They had meant something, and then they were forced to live past that: through a terrible time of meaning nothing, of knowing they could now only be the beneficiaries of younger people's patience.

"The Resolution is a celebration of life—we can end our lives with dignity.

"It is a time of transition. One generation handing the responsibilities of life to the next . . ."

What Ambassador Troi gained from losing a friend to the Resolution was the understanding: "Ritual provides a structure for a society . . . good rituals, bad rituals alike."

# BETAZOIDS

Unlike their fellow telepaths the Vulcans, Betazoids are explosive with emotions. They enjoy everything life has to offer, and if you ever get the chance to spend some time with any, their infectious love of life may just rub off on you. Their telepathic abilities are natural, developing in adolescence. The Betazoids tend to speak to each other telepathically, though some believe this to be rude behavior, especially in front of nontelepaths.

## Everyday Rituals

Their telepathic nature mandates a certain level of meditation. One form of Betazoid meditation may make a person appear

dead, but through the relaxation techniques and burning candles, one can attain peace and be "at one with the All Being."
Practitioners believe it to be a wonderful procedure that can center you.

A traditional form of thanksgiving, though not widely practiced, is the ringing of chimes. After every bite of food, a chime is
struck, providing for a loud meal, if not an entertaining one.

## Weddings

It has been said that Betazoid weddings are "widely regarded as
the most beautiful in the universe." And who better to say something like this than Lwaxana Troi, the Heir to the Holy Rings of
Betazed, Holder of the Sacred Chalice of Rixx, who herself has
been married multiple times.

Children are often genetically bonded at a young age to a mate
chosen by their parents. It is expected that they will marry when
they reach a certain age, but it is not unheard of that the intended
wedding doesn't take place.

One of the many grand traditions of these weddings is that
Betazoid brides wear no clothes. To a non-Betazoid this can be
unnerving, particularly if one is unaware of the tradition that
calls for *all* guests to attend the festivities unclothed. The lack of
attire is intended to honor the act of love being celebrated. The
participants bare everything, hiding nothing, in order to support
the love of the couple.

## KTARIANS

The Ktarians have a rough history with Starfleet. Their attempt to
gain control of Starfleet through an addictive game put them at
odds with this organization. But this was the work of one group.

Ktarians have strong family bonds. A familiar Ktarian custom is to name a child after a relative, much as Earth humans have been known to do over the centuries.

## Death Rituals

Ktarians have a specific death, or funeral, ritual. On their home of Ktaria VII, within the burial tombs, they place thousands of nondescript stones. These are, however, sacred stones, each representing a special prayer for the deceased from those they leave behind.

# JEM'HADAR

"Obedience brings victory and victory is life."

Obedience is the key to the Jem'Hadar; of course, it was genetically engineered into them. They were bred to fight, nothing more, nothing less. Their instincts kick in within days of birth. It was a biologically "programmed" addiction to ketracel-white that kept them going. That is how the Founders engineered them to function.

Their addiction to ketracel-white, an isogenic enzyme, forced them into a daily ritual of ingestion. A Vorta assigned to control and command a Jem'Hadar group would produce the material and they would line up at attention . . . waiting. They would pledge their allegiance:

"We pledge our loyalty to the Founders for now until death."

"The Founders are like gods to the Jem'Hadar," a Jem'Hadar First, the leader of a group, was quoted as saying, "but our gods never talk to us and they don't wait for us after death. They only want us to fight for them . . . and die for them."

Klingons will fight to the death, but they take great joy in victory; the Jem'Hadar acceptance of the inevitability of death could be unnerving:

> "I am First. And I am dead. As of this moment, we are all dead.
>
> "We go into battle to win back our lives. This we do gladly because we are Jem'Hadar. Remember, victory is life."

With their lives pledged to service to the Founders, failing one in any way, especially allowing a Founder to die—as happened on Torga IV in the Gamma Quadrant—will cause the Jem'Hadar to kill themselves. The ritual suicide is the only response they can conceive of for disappointing their gods.

## VORTA

Many of the Vorta were, for lack of a better word, cruel to the Jem'Hadar they were responsible for. The ironic truth of the situation was that they were in the same situation—the Vorta serve the Founder in all things. The Vorta were clones. A failure or a flaw would result in termination of the clone and the activation of the next clone in the series. They, too, were genetically specific to what the Founders needed: no sense of smell or color, which left little to distract them, but their excellent hearing fulfilled a vital need of the Founders.

According to legend, the connection between Vortas and Founders can be traced back to a family of primitive Vorta who once hid a shapeshifter from an angry mob of solids. This shapeshifter was so grateful for their actions that he promised that one day the Vorta would be important and powerful interstellar beings. When the shapeshifters rose to power as the Founders, they genetically engineered the Vorta into their present form.

## FOUNDERS

Once, the Founders freely explored the galaxy, using their shapeshifting abilities to fit into any society and environment.

Then solids began hunting them and they settled in the Gamma Quadrant, sending out a hundred infants to continue exploring. Deep Space 9 Security Chief Odo discovered he was one of these infants.

The fear that the Founders infused in the Alpha Quadrant during the Dominion War—you never knew where or who a shapeshifter could be—pushed the combined forces of the Federation, Klingons, and Romulans to the edge. The toll the war took on the Alpha, Beta, and Gamma Quadrants is still being tabulated.

Through the link, shapeshifters connect to one another. This fluid form is their natural state. As Odo explained to the shapeshifter Laas, the linking involved "a melding into one—the merging of thought and form, idea and sensation."

The link is what shapeshifters are; it offers them the true meaning of existence. This is the way they get their information, the way they learn, the way they live.

# ANDORIANS

The Andorians describe themselves as passionate, violent people. They have been active in the Federation for centuries. An Andorian was even up for the Federation's coveted and prestigious Carrington Award, Starfleet's highest medical honor.

## Weddings

It has been reported that Andorian marriages require groups of four people. This could be a reflection of their admitted passion, or a strong showing of community. There is another ceremony that allows for just two people to wed, much like a traditional human wedding, but little is known of that version.

# BREEN

One of the most warlike species to be engaged in battle, the Breen have left their mark on the Federation. Though they claimed political nonalignment, the Breen sided with the Dominion during that war. The Romulans, who themselves are nothing to sneeze at in battle, have a saying when dealing with the Breen:

Never turn your back on a Breen.

# TAMARIANS

Commander Data provided some background on Tamarian people. "The children of Tama were called 'incomprehensible' by Captain Silvestri of the *Shikar Maru*. Other accounts were comparable.

"The Tamarian ego structure does not seem to allow what we normally think of as self-identity," Data informed. "Their ability to abstract is highly unusual. They seem to communicate through narrative imagery—by reference to the individual and places which appear in their mytho-historical accounts."

Captain Picard witnessed a ritual that seemed more habit than custom when the Tamarian captain he had encountered alternated between picking up one or more objects removed from his own uniform and then dropping them on the ground, touching his forehead after their fall. His manner was not particularly religious.

Picard was able to report some success in reaching an understanding with this captain, who had initiated the meeting. The Tamarian's unique verbal dynamics made it difficult at first, but once Picard comprehended the linguistic metaphor system, he was able to decipher the Tamarian tale of "Darmok and Jalad at Tanagra."

Darmok on the ocean.
Tanagra on the ocean. Darmok at Tanagra.
Jalad on the ocean. Jalad at Tanagra.
The beast at Tanagra.
Darmok and Jalad at Tanagra.

Picard was able to translate:

Darmok was alone on the ocean and went to the
island, Tanagra. Jalad also went to the island.

> Together, they fought the beast that lived on the
> island, and they left together.

The Tamarian was telling Picard that their situation was similar, that danger shared can sometimes bring two people together. Darmok and Jalad at Tanagra. Picard and Dathon at El-Adrel IV.

It was through this meeting that Picard was able to bring the Federation one giant leap closer in communication with this people. For now, we are all

> Tembra . . . his arms wide.

Or:

> Trying to find out more.

## TALAXIANS

The Talaxians are a hospitable, Delta Quadrant life-form who enjoy life, despite a decade-long war with the Haakonian Order. As part of their philosophy of embracing all aspects of life, it is traditional to share the history of a meal before you begin eating, as a way of enhancing the culinary experience. Every course, every little bit of food was enhanced by the verbal garnish.

### *Prixin*

Family is central to Talaxian lives, and *Prixin* is celebrated annually by the family. A lavish feast is prepared, and a common room is brightly and festively decorated with tree branches and a small sculpture of the guiding tree. The traditional salutation is long, but even when broken up, by not completing the full list of familial connections, it showcases the Talaxian family spirit.

"Welcome to the First Night of *Prixin*—the Talaxian observance of familial allegiance. We do not stand alone, we are in the arms of family. Father, mother, sister, brother, father's father, father's mother, father's brother, mother's brother . . .

"We gather on this day to extol the warmth and joy of those unshakable bonds.

"Without them, we could not call ourselves complete.

"On this day we are thankful to be together.

"We do not stand alone."

## The Guiding Tree

Even after death, Talaxian myth does not allow one to stand alone. Waiting for the Talaxian after he or she dies is the guiding tree. It stands at the center of the Talaxian afterlife deep inside the Great Forest. The guiding tree is there to help one find the way after arrival in the Great Forest. It is at the guiding tree where the gathering of ancestors takes place, where everyone who has gone on before would be to meet the newly arrived.

## Death Rituals

Talaxians mourn their dead for a full week in a specific burial ceremony. The guiding tree is central here, with family supporting the travels of the newly departed to the Great Forest.

## VHNORI

A sophisticated race, in an undisclosed location, the Vhnori had very specific thoughts on death. Their belief is that they would

simply move onto a higher level of consciousness and be reunited with family in the afterlife.

## Death Rituals

Within an exotic-looking chamber filled with technology, artifacts, and inscriptions; it's a mortuary and it's high-tech and very ceremonial.

An oval pod, the size of one body, is the focus of the room. Vhnori gather around the pod; they are dressed in ceremonial clothing. There is an upbeat feeling to the ceremony; they have just sent one of their loved ones into the afterlife.

A Vhnori, dressed more distinctively, speaks. "Death is the end of this life, but it is also the beginning of a new journey. Ptera (the newly deceased) will now thrive in the Next Emanation. This is both her sacred duty and her great privilege."

The gathered answered, "*Eler'atah.*"

The officiator continued, "As she begins her transition, we promise to carry memories of her so that when we enter the—"

Unfortunately, the realization that Harry Kim is inside the pod disrupted their ritual.

One of the Vhnori later explained to Kim. "My people have come to think of death as just another stage of our existence. There are some people who are ever eager to die. If they feel depressed or lonely in this life, they simply go on to the next one [life]."

The Vhnori, Hatil, has a medical brace on his body and acknowledged, "Ever since the accident, life hasn't been easy, but I have to say this [death] is more my family's idea than it is mine. I'm a burden to them right now. It takes a lot of their time and resources to care for me, and I can't give much back to them.

"So there was a family meeting, and it was agreed that I should move on to the Next Emanation," he explained to Kim.

"It's not my place to judge your culture," the shocked ensign noted. "But from my perspective, it's a little . . . chilling to hear that."

"Well . . . even though the family did it out of love, and everyone was happy for me and said they'd see me when *they* got to the Next Emanation, I have to admit there is a little voice inside me that is terrified of dying," Hatil admitted. "And since I've been talking to you, that little voice has started to get louder."

Still, Hatil decided to follow his family's wishes. His body is completely covered in the ceremonial shroud. "A pleasant trip, Hatil," his wife said. "Say hello to Varel and Toyan. I'll see you there in a few years."

An officiator comes to lead the ceremony. "We are joined here today to bid farewell to our dear friend Hatil Garan. We salute not only his life, but also the manner in which he has chosen to end it. He makes a noble sacrifice today, so that his family may have a better tomorrow.

"We prepare to send him into the Next Emanation with the full knowledge and faith that the life he will find there is better than the one here. That he will no longer be hampered by his infirmity and that he will understand the cosmos in a way he could never have imagined."

# TAVNIANS

## Weddings

In a Tavnian wedding, the groom has to stand before the bride and tell her why he wants to marry her. He must proclaim his love for her and convince her to accept him as her husband, in the presence of family and friends. If anyone doubts the groom's sincerity, that person can challenge the marriage.

A ceremonial pedestal is set in the center of a room. The groom is dressed in Tavnian wedding tunic. The barefoot bride wears a lush and flowing Tavnian wedding gown. She carries a traditional Tavnian light ball and steps up onto the pedestal.

The groom states his intentions.

In a ceremony that took place on Deep Space 9, the vows were as follows:

In keeping with Tavnian tradition, I stand before you, here in my home, among my worldly possessions, in order to declare my wish to add this woman to that which is mine. She is as kind as she is beautiful, and I want her to be part of my life from this day on. Marry me.

The groom may be called upon to justify his intentions if the marriage is questioned. The response, as spoken here by Odo, may be something like:

Before I met her, my world was a much smaller place. I kept to myself. I didn't need anyone else, and I took pride in that.

The truth is, I was ashamed of what I was, afraid if people saw how truly different I was, they would recoil from me.

She saw how different I was, but she didn't recoil. She wanted to see more.

For the first time in my life, someone wanted me as I was. And that changed me forever.

The day I met her is the day I stopped being alone.

And I want her to be part of my life from this day on.

Having convinced everyone present, the groom reaches his hand up to the bride and speaks the ritual words to complete the ceremony:

Marry me, let me into your light.

The bride offers her hand to him, and he joins her on the pedestal and says:

> I give myself to you, forever and always.

The groom announces:

> I say for all to hear that this woman is mine. If anyone challenges my claim to her, let them do so now.

# SEVEN

# Food for Thought and Holiday Happenings

In order to properly cater the wide variety of events that take place in the United Federation of Planets, one must consider all the various palates that are to be satisfied.

In the case of the wedding of Worf and Jadzia Dax, a Klingon selection was the selection since the Trill bride had a great fondness for all thing Klingon. But you might want to consider your guest before settling on Klingon skull stew as the main dish.

One can start the festivities with a staple of Klingon food-stuffs: *gagh*, the wormlike treat you can eat with your hands. A double main course of skull stew and heart of *targ* would certainly please the in-laws . . . especially if their wedding gift is a pair of matching *bat'leths*. But remember, maybe a Trill would also request her favorite meal, the vegetarian Azna. The Klingon groom might offer up his human mother's version of *rokeg* blood pie.

A constant that seems to permeate Starfleet is a love of choco-late, so the wedding cake should be chocolate, and the more the better. The beverage service would have bloodwine; Worf's drink of choice, prune juice; and the popular coffee blend of *raktajino*, Klingon coffee with a kick.

Yridian brandy, which is always saved for a special occasion, would toast the bride and groom . . . after the painstik attack, nat-urally.

"Anything worth doing in a holosuite can be done better in the real world," Kira tells Quark.

"You obviously haven't been in the right holosuite program," Quark responds.

The holosuites and the holodecks are an important aspect of Starfleet life. In fact, even though Kira said this to Quark, she did get caught up in holosuite fun (as long as Jadzia Dax dragged her along). But the holodeck and suites could be used for healing purposes; for sport, racquetball is quite popular. Worf and Dax used them for Klingon calisthenics. But, more often than not, one could find literary characters come to life, ancient Earth establishments like Las Vegas lounges, or a 1950s private eye.

A day spent in a holodeck could take people away from everything around them, making them forget their troubles.

> "All things considered," Ezri says, "I'd rather be on Risa."
>
> "That makes two of us," agrees Sisko.

Two of the most popular vacation destinations in the Federation are the pleasure planet of Risa and the shores of the Janaeran Falls on Betazed.

Betazed is a lush world where the natives are telepaths, but that shouldn't discourage anyone from visiting this paradise of optimism and tranquility. Even some of the native foods, like *oskoid,* a leafy finger food that's a Betazoid delicacy, and Arcturian Fizz, which has certain pleasure-enhancing qualities, just add to the experience.

Risa is the epitome of hedonistic pleasure. All you can eat, drink, and play—in all forms—is available to visitors. Champagne and Delvin fluff pastries are just a request away. Everything about Risa is about getting away from it all. This place beats out any holodeck.

When Worf first arrives at DS9, he goes to the bar,
and Quark looks at the new arrival and says, "Let me
guess, Klingon bloodwine."

But Worf surpises him, "Prune juice, chilled."

Keeping bar on a space station is no easy matter, what with tar-
iffs and various species' choosy tastes. Quark does the best he
can, as only a Ferengi can, and keeps Quark's Bar, Grill, Gaming
House, and Holosuite Arcade (a wholly owned subsidary of
Quark Enterprises, Inc.) up and running.

To whet your whistle after intergalactic travel, you might
order a frosty Bajoran ale or the specially concocted Black
Hole. You can get Klingon bloodwine or basic synthehol.
*Kanar*, a Cardassian beverage, is in good supply there
because . . . Quark was under the impression the Cardassians
might be back "someday." Other species' favorite drinks are
covered and in good supply like Aldorian ale, Andonian tea,
and Tamarin froth.

Food is also plentiful at Quark's, where one can get the simple
and appetizer-like Gramilian sand peas with *yamok* sauce or the
full meal of kilm steak and mashed potatoes with butter . . . if one
is so inclined.

"What'll you have, Commander?" Quark asks the
new station commander.

"How's the local synthale?" Sisko replies.

"You won't like it," Quark says, and then quickly
adds, "I love the Bajorans, such a deeply spiritual culture, but they make a dreadful ale."

Ferengi have a particular palate, but when Rom started working for the Bajoran militia and *not* his brother, his tastes changed. Instead of his normal breakfast of puree of beetle, Rom chose a human, Chief O'Brien's, normal fare, which is two (chicken) eggs over easy with three strips of bacon and a side of corned beef hash—which totally disgusts Quark . . . who goes back to his own raw slug livers.

One of the most interesting places to find an assortment of foods and life-forms would be Earth, where the headquarters of Starfleet can be found. A planet with multiple cultures, Earth is the homeworld of the best-known captains in Starfleet history.

If a senior staff of a starship were to sit down to a meal, a Federation potluck so to speak, what would they bring? If the captain provides the drink, let's take a look at possible choices . . .

"Beware Romulans bearing gifts. Happy Birthday, Jim," McCoy tells Kirk, who opens the gift.

"Romulan ale? Why, Bones, you know this is illegal."

"I only use it for medicinal purposes," McCoy defends.

## Beverages

The beverage choices within the Federation are as wide-ranging as the life-forms. There is something for everything. Some of the better-known selections are: root beer, Fanalian toddy (served hot), Til'amin froth beverage, single Irish malt whisky, neat, Aldebaran whiskey, Andorian ale, Alvanian brandy, brestanti ale, Calaman sherry, Romulan ale, synthehol, Arcturian Fizz (which has certain pleasure-enhancing qualities), Muskan seed punch, nectar direct from Prometheus, iced coffee, *raktajino,* coffee, champagne, and more tea than you can shake a painstik at—Earl Grey, Tarkalean (soothing), *Jestral,* Maruvian, Gavaline.

If we were to use suggestions from Deanna Troi and Kira Nerys for dessert, they would bring chocolate cake and Delvin fluff pastries. Jake Sisko would sneak some *jumja* candy and I'danian pudding onto the table. Jadzia Dax's favorite dish was Andorian tuber root as a good side. Quark, if invited, could bring the popular Alterian chowder, a well-replicated meal soup. Going all out, the O'Briens could take the time to make a *q'parol* casserole. Another soup brought to the table could be the traditional *plomeek* soup of Vulcan, by Tuvok. One thing to note of our menu so far is that it's primarily vegetarian. Captain Sisko, a wonderful cook, could have made a shrimp Creole for his offering. Pasta al Fiorella would come out of the replicator of Geordi La Forge. Riker, on the other hand, could dig up *gagh,* Cardassian style, with *yamok* sauce, a good mix of cultures between Klingon and Cardassian cuisines. Worf might bring Petrokian sausage . . . for a change. Tom Paris would certainly bring pizza, his favorite. Chakotay could find a way to have *angla'bosque* there.

That's a pretty good spread, if you sit back and look at it . . . and don't expect too much meat. There is, of course, a wide range of foods available to these Starfleet officers and personnel, and even without those not even mentioned here, you would still have plenty to choose from.

If you scan the Starfleet database you can see the importance of food in understanding life-forms. Aside from the Earth custom of shaking hands, to show your weapon hand is empty, there is no better way to see how a people see themselves.

Gul Dukat has a lot of problems with the Bajorans who have come in and taken over his space station, but he notes, "You do know how to make a perfect onion soup."

The Romulan commander informs then Commander Spock that "I've had special Vulcan dishes prepared for you. I hope they're to your liking."

"I'm very flattered, Commander. There is no doubt that the cuisine aboard our vessel is far superior to that of the *Enterprise*," he says and then reacts, "It is indeed a very powerful recruitment inducement."

"There's an ancient Chinese curse, Captain: 'May you live in interesting times . . .' Mealtime is always 'interesting' now that Neelix is in the kitchen." Janeway smiles. "We shouldn't judge him too harshly. He is helping us conserve replicator energy . . ."

"And I'm sure the gastrointestinal problems will go away as soon as our systems get used to his gourmet touch," Paris observes.

Janeway is a bit perturbed at Neelix's ease when dealing with her, but she decides to forgive him this time out for a bigger problem. "Do we have any coffee left?"

"No, but we have something even better . . ."

She frowns. "I don't want something even better. I want coffee."

Neelix, though, is excited. "Really, it's made from a proteinaceous seed I discovered on an expedition to the fourth moon of . . ."

Janeway, in a way, brushes him off. "Never mind. I'll use one of my replicator rations for coffee."

She's stopped in her tracks by his response: "That would not be appropriate, Captain."

"I beg your pardon?"

"You need to set an example for the crew," Neelix informs her.

"Well, thank you for reminding me . . ."

"You're welcome. After all, if you want the crew to begin to accept natural food alternatives instead of further depleting our energy reserves, you have to encourage them by your own choices, don't you?" He puts this all out, and it seems the captain is less than pleased.

"Fine, give me your 'even better' than coffee substitute . . ."

"And how about some Takar loggerhead eggs with that this morning?"

"Just coffee."

Neelix pours the even-better-than-coffee, and it comes out of the pot like syrup. "It's a tiny bit richer blend than you're used to, but you'll learn to love it."

"One day a week, that's all I ask," Paris moaned to Neelix. "How hard can it be?"

"Harder than you think," Neelix informed him.

"Neelix, it's *pizza*. Bread, tomatoes, cheese."

"The cheese alone would take days," Neelix explained. "Spreading curds and whey from synthesized milk is a delicate process."

Deanna Troi was partaking of a chocolate sundae composed of chocolate ice cream, fudge, and chips. "You're not depressed, are you?" a concerned Riker asked.

"I'm fine, Commander." But she was a bit embarrassed. "I never met chocolate I didn't like."

Her hesitation on eating the sundae struck Riker as odd. "Doesn't it taste good?"

"Of course it does. But it's not just a matter of taste. It's the whole experience." She explained and demonstrated. "First you spoon the fudge from around the rim, leaving only the ice cream in the middle. Then gently spoon the ice cream around the sides, like you're sculpting it. Relish every bite. Make every one an event. And on the last bite, close your eyes."

"I never knew it was such a ritual," Riker reacted.

"Chocolate is a serious thing," Troi stated.

Scotty approached Chekov and asked, "When are you going to get off that mild diet, lad?"

Chekov raised his drink. "This is vodka."

"Where I come from, that's soda pop," Scotty taunted. "Now, this is a drink for a man."

"Scotch?"

"Aye," Scotty said.

"It was invented by a little old lady from Leningrad," Chekov huffed.

"Excuse me, sir," Rand interrupted Captain Kirk. "It's past time you had something to eat." She handed him some food.

"What the devil is this? Green leaves?"

"Dietary salad, sir," she told him. "Dr. McCoy ordered your diet card changed. I thought you knew."

McCoy explained, "Your weight was up a couple of pounds, remember?"

Kirk turned to Rand. "Bring some for the doctor, too."

. . .

"There's coffee in that nebula," Janeway tells Chakotay on their new course setting.

# ACKNOWLEDGMENTS

Thanks to the following photographers: Bryce Birmelin 13, 73, 81; Bryon J. Cohen 68; Danny Feld 129, 141; Elliot Marks, 2, 10; Robbie Robinson 8, 15, 18, 22, 24, 30, 33, 35, 39, 45, 48, 51, 53, 60, 64, 71, 86, 89, 91, 97, 99, 101, 106, 112, 116, 122, 124, 127, 132, 134, 136, 138, 140, 144, 148, 149, 150, 153, 155, 157, 181

And special thanks to Margaret and Marco for everything; for Jim Catapano for use of his brain and eyes; to Dave McD, Eddie B, and Mike Mac for *Star Trek* training; and to Mom and Dad, my first editors.

# BIBLIOGRAPHY

The works listed here were used in the creation of the publication. The author recognizes and appreciates the work that went into each and every item.

*Star Trek Federation Travel Guide* by Michael Jan Friedman

*The Star Trek Encyclopedia: A Reference Guide to the Future* by Denise and Michael Okuda

*The Klingon Way: A Warrior's Guide* by Marc Okrand

*Quotable Star Trek* by Jill Sherwin

*Star Trek Cookbook* by Ethan Philips and William J. Birnes

*Star Trek: Deep Space Nine—Legends of the Ferengi* by Ira Steven Behr and Robert Hewitt Wolfe


*Star Trek: The Motion Picture.* Screenplay by Harold Livingston. Story by Alan Dean Foster. Directed by Robert Wise.

*Star Trek II: The Wrath Of Khan.* Screenplay by Jack B. Sowards. Story by Harve Bennett and Jack B. Sowards. Directed by Nicholas Meyer.

*Star Trek III: The Search For Spock.* Written by Harve Bennett. Directed by Leonard Nimoy.

*Star Trek: First Contact.* Screenplay by Brannon Braga & Ronald D. Moore. Story by Rick Berman & Brannon Braga & Ronald D. Moore. Directed by Jonathan Frakes.

*Star Trek Generations.* Screenplay by Ronald D. Moore & Brannon Braga. Story by Rick Berman & Ronald D. Moore & Brannon Braga. Directed by David Carson.

*Star Trek: Insurrection.* Screenplay by Michael Piller. Story by Rick Berman & Michael Piller. Directed by Jonathan Frakes.

# Bibliography

## Star Trek

"Amok Time." Written by Theodore Sturgeon. Directed by Joseph Pevney.

"Balance Of Terror." Written by Paul Schneider. Directed by Vincent McEveety.

"Day Of The Dove." Written by Jerome Bixby. Directed by Marvin Chomsky.

"Elaan Of Troyius." Written and Directed by John Meredyth Lucas.

"The *Enterprise* Incident." Written by D. C. Fontana. Directed by John Meredyth Lucas.

"For the World Is Hollow and I Have Touched the Sky." Written by Rik Vollaerts. Directed by Tony Leader.

"Journey to Babel." Written by D. C. Fontana. Directed by Joseph Pevney.

"The Paradise Syndrome." Written by Margaret Armen. Directed by Jud Taylor.

"The Return of the Archons." Teleplay by Boris Sobelman. Story by Gene Roddenberry. Directed by Joseph Pevney.

"Whom Gods Destroy." Teleplay by Lee Erwin. Story by Lee Erwin and Jerry Sohl. Directed by Herb Wallerstein.

## Star Trek: The Next Generation

"All Good Things . . ." Written by Ronald D. Moore & Brannon Braga. Directed by Winrich Kolbe.

"Allegiance." Written by Richard Manning & Hans Beimler. Directed by Winrich Kolbe.

"The Bonding." Written by Ronald D. Moore. Directed by Winrich Kolbe.

"Chain of Command," Part I & II. Part 1 Teleplay by Ronald D. Moore. Story by Frank Abatemarco. Directed by Robert Scheerer. Part 2 Written by Frank Abatemarco. Directed by Les Landau.

"The Child." Written by Jaron Summers & Jon Povill and Maurice Hurley. Directed by Rob Bowman.

"Conspiracy." Teleplay by Tracy Tormé. Story by Robert Sabaroff. Directed by Cliff Bole.

"Cost of Living." Written by Peter Allan Fields. Directed by Winrich Kolbe.

"Datalore." Teleplay by Robert Lewin and Gene Roddenberry. Story by Robert Lewin and Maurice Hurley. Directed by Rob Bowman.

# Bibliography

"Data's Day." Teleplay by Harold Apter and Ronald D. Moore. Story by Harold Apter. Directed by Robert Wiemer.

"Darmok." Teleplay by Joe Menosky. Story by Philip LaZebnik and Joe Menosky. Directed by Winrich Kolbe.

"The Dauphin." Written by Scott Rubenstein & Leonard Mlodinow. Directed by Robert Bowman.

"The Emissary." Television story and Teleplay by Richard Manning & Hans Beimler. Based on an unpublished story by Thomas H. Calder. Directed by Cliff Bole.

"Encounter At Farpoint." Written by D. C. Fontana and Gene Roddenberry. Directed by Corey Allen.

"Ethics." Teleplay by Ronald D. Moore. Story by Sara Charno & Stuart Charno. Directed by Chip Chalmers.

"Evolution." Teleplay by Michael Piller. Story by Michael Piller and Michael Wagner. Directed by Winrich Kolbe.

"Firstborn." Teleplay by René Echevarria. Story by Mark Kalbfeld. Directed by Jonathan West.

"Gambit" Part II. Teleplay by Ronald D. Moore. Story by Naren Shankar. Directed by Alexander Singer.

"The Game." Teleplay by Brannon Braga. Story by Susan Sackett & Fred Bronson and Brannon Braga. Directed by Corey Allen.

"Half a Life." Teleplay by Peter Allan Fields. Story by Ted Roberts and Peter Allan Fields. Directed by Les Landau.

"Haven." Teleplay by Tracy Tormé. Story by Tracy Tormé & Lan Okun. Directed by Richard Compton.

"Heart of Glory." Teleplay by Maurice Hurley. Story by Maurice Hurley and Herbert Wright & D. C. Fontana. Directed by Rob Bowman.

"Hero Worship." Teleplay by Joe Menosky. Story by Hilary J. Bader. Directed by Patrick Stewart.

"The Icarus Factor." Teleplay by David Assael and Robert L. McCullough. Story by David Assael. Directed by Robert Iscove.

"Interface." Written by Joe Menosky. Directed by Robert Wiemer.

"Journey's End." Written by Ronald D. Moore. Directed by Corey Allen.

"Manhunt." Written by Terry Devereaux. Directed by Rob Bowman.

# Bibliography

"Ménage à Troi." Written by Fred Bronson & Susan Sackett. Directed by Rob Legato.

"The Next Phase." Written by Ronald D. Moore. Directed by David Carson.

"Parallels." Written by Brannon Braga. Directed by Robert Wiemer.

"Phantasms." Written by Brannon Braga. Directed by Patrick Stewart.

"Peak Performance." Written by David Kemper. Directed by Robert Scheerer.

"The Perfect Mate." Teleplay by Gary Perconte and Michael Piller. Story by René Echevarria and Gary Perconte. Directed by Cliff Bole.

"Power Play." Teleplay by Rene Balcer and Herbert J. Wright & Brannon Braga. Story by Paul Reuben and Maurice Hurley. Directed by David Livingston.

"QPid." Teleplay by Ira Steven Behr. Story by Randee Russell and Ira Steven Behr. Directed by Cliff Bole.

"Redemption" Parts I & II. Written by Ronald D. Moore. Part 1 Directed by Cliff Bole. Part 2 Directed by David Carson.

"Reunion." Teleplay by Thomas Perry & Jo Perry and Ronald D. Moore & Brannon Braga. Story by Drew Deighan and Thomas Perry & Jo Perry. Directed by Jonathan Frakes.

"Rightful Heir." Teleplay by Ronald D. Moore. Story by James E. Brooks. Directed by Winrich Kolbe.

"Sins of the Father." Teleplay by Ronald D. Moore & W. Reed Moran. Based on a teleplay by Drew Deighan. Directed by Les Landau.

"Suddenly Human." Teleplay by John Whelpley & Jeri Taylor. Story by Ralph Phillips. Directed by Gabrielle Beaumont.

"The Survivors." Written by Michael Wagner. Directed by Les Landau.

"Thine Own Self." Teleplay by Ronald D. Moore. Story by Christopher Hatton. Directed by Winrich Kolbe.

"Transfigurations." Written by René Echevarria. Directed by Tom Benko.

"Unification." Part 1 Teleplay by Jeri Taylor. Story by Rick Berman & Michael Piller. Directed by Les Landau. Part 2 Teleplay by Michael Piller. Story by Rick Berman & Michael Piller. Directed by Cliff Bole.

"Up the Long Ladder." Written by Melinda M. Snodgrass. Directed by Winrich Kolbe.

"Where No One Has Gone Before." Written by Diane Duane & Michael Reaves. Directed by Rob Bowman.

## Star Trek: Deep Space Nine

"The Abandoned." Written by D. Thomas Maio & Steve Warnek. Directed by Avery Brooks.

"The Adversary." Written by Ira Steven Behr & Robert Hewitt Wolfe. Directed by Alexander Singer.

"Afterimage." Written by René Echevarria. Directed by Les Landau.

"The Alternate." Teleplay by Bill Dial. Story by Jim Trombetta and Bill Dial. Directed by David Carson.

"Apocalypse Rising." Written by Ira Steven Behr & Robert Hewitt Wolfe. Directed by James L. Conway.

"The Assignment." Teleplay by David Weddle & Bradley Thompson. Story by David R. Long & Robert Lederman. Directed by Allan Kroeker.

"The Begotten." Written by René Echevarria. Directed by Jesus Salvador Treviño.

"Body Parts." Teleplay by Hans Beimler. Story by Louis P. DeSantis & Robert J. Bolivar. Directed by Avery Brooks.

"Call To Arms." Written by Ira Steven Behr & Robert Hewitt Wolfe. Directed by Allan Kroeker.

"Chimera." Written by René Echevarria. Directed by Steve Posey.

"The Darkness and the Light." Teleplay by Ronald D. Moore. Story by Bryan Fuller. Directed by Michael Vejar.

"Doctor Bashir, I Presume?" Teleplay by Ronald D. Moore. Story by Jimmy Diggs. Directed by David Livingston.

"Dogs of War." Teleplay by René Echevarria & Ronald D. Moore. Story by Peter Allan Fields. Directed by Avery Brooks.

"Emissary" Parts I & II. Teleplay by Michael Piller. Story by Rick Berman & Michael Piller. Directed by David Carson.

"Facets." Written by René Echevarria. Directed by Cliff Bole.

"Family Business." Written by Ira Steven Behr & Robert Hewitt Wolfe. Directed by Rene Auberjonois.

"Fascination." Teleplay by Philip LaZebnik. Story by Ira Steven Behr & James Crocker. Directed by Avery Brooks.

"Ferengi Love Songs." Written by Ira Steven Behr & Hans Beimler. Directed by René Auberjonois.

"Heart of Stone." Written by Ira Steven Behr & Robert Hewitt Wolfe. Directed by Alexander Singer.

"Hippocratic Oath." Teleplay by Lisa Klink. Story by Nicholas Corea and Lisa Klink. Directed by Rene Auberjonois.

"The House of Quark." Teleplay by Ronald D. Moore. Story by Tom Benko. Directed by Les Landau.

"Image in the Sand." Written by Ira Steven Behr & Hans Beimler. Directed by Les Landau.

"Indiscretion." Teleplay by Nicholas Corea. Story by Toni Marberry & Jack Treviño. Directed by LeVar Burton.

"The Jem'Hadar." Written by Ira Steven Behr. Directed by Kim Friedman.

"Let He Who Is Without Sin . . ." Written by Robert Hewitt Wolfe & Ira Steven Behr. Directed by Rene Auberjonois.

"Looking for *par'Mach* in All the Wrong Places." Written by Ronald D. Moore. Directed by Andrew J. Robinson.

"Melora." Teleplay by Evan Carlos Somers and Steven Baum and Michael Piller & James Crocker. Story by Evan Carlos Somers. Directed by Winrich Kolbe.

"Meridian." Teleplay by Mark Gehred-O'Connell. Story by Hilary Bader and Evan Carlos Somers. Directed by Jonathan Frakes.

"The Muse." Teleplay by René Echevarria. Story by René Echevarria and Majel Barrett-Roddenberry. Directed by David Livingston.

"The Nagus." Teleplay by Ira Steven Behr. Story by David Livingston. Directed by David Livingston.

"Our Man Bashir." Teleplay by Ronald D. Moore. Story by Robert Gillan. Directed by Winrich Kolbe.

"Penumbra." Written by René Echevarria. Directed by Steve Posey.

"Playing God." Teleplay by Jim Trombetta and Michael Piller. Story by Jim Trombetta. Directed by David Livingston.

"The Reckoning." Teleplay by David Weddle & Bradley Thompson. Story by Harry M. Werksman & Gabrielle Stanton. Directed by Jesus Salvador Treviño.

# Bibliography

"Rejoined." Teleplay by Ronald D. Moore & René Echevarria. Story by René Echevarria. Directed by Avery Brooks.

"Rivals." Teleplay by Joe Menosky. Story by Jim Trombetta and Michael Piller. Directed by David Livingston.

"The Search" Parts I & II. Part I Teleplay by Ronald D. Moore. Story by Ira Steven Behr & Robert Hewitt Wolfe. Directed by Kim Friedman. Part II Teleplay by Ira Steven Behr. Story by Ira Steven Behr & Robert Hewitt Wolfe. Directed by Jonathan Frakes.

"Shadows and Symbols." Written by Ira Steven Behr & Hans Beimler. Directed by Allan Kroeker.

"Shakaar." Written by Gordon Dawson. Directed by Jonathan West.

"Sound of Her Voice." Teleplay by Ronald D. Moore. Story by Pam Pietroforte. Directed by Winrich Kolbe.

"Sons of Mogh." Written by Ronald D. Moore. Directed by David Livingston.

"Starship Down." Written by David Mack & John J. Ordover. Directed by Alexander Singer.

"Strange Bedfellows." Written by Ronald D. Moore. Directed by Rene Auberjonois.

"The Sword of Kahless." Teleplay by Hans Beimler. Story by Richard Danus. Directed by LeVar Burton.

"Tacking into the Wind." Written by Ronald D. Moore. Directed by Mike Vejar.

"Tears of the Prophets." Written by Ira Steven Behr & Hans Beimler. Directed by Allan Kroeker.

"Ties of Blood and Water." Teleplay by Robert Hewitt Wolfe. Story by Edmund Newton & Robbin L. Slocum. Directed by Avery Brooks.

" 'Til Death Do Us Part." Written by David Weddle & Bradley Thompson. Directed by Winrich Kolbe.

"To the Death." Written by Ira Steven Behr & Robert Hewitt Wolfe. Directed by LeVar Burton.

"Treachery, Faith and the Great River." Teleplay by David Weddle & Bradley Thompson. Story by Philip Kim. Directed by Steve Posey.

"The Way of the Warrior." Written by Ira Steven Behr & Robert Hewitt Wolfe. Directed by James L. Conway.

"What You Leave Behind." Written by Ira Steven Behr & Hans Beimler. Directed by Allan Kroeker.

"When It Rains." Teleplay by René Echevarria. Story by René Echevarria & Spike Steingasser. Directed by Michael Dorn.

"You Are Cordially Invited." Written by Ronald D. Moore. Directed by David Livingston.

## Star Trek: Voyager

"Alter Ego." Written by Joe Menosky. Directed by Robert Picardo.

"Barge of the Dead." Teleplay by Bryan Fuller. Story by Ronald D. Moore and Bryan Fuller. Directed by Mike Vejar.

"Before and After." Written by Kenneth Biller. Directed by Allan Kroeker.

"Blood Fever." Written by Lisa Klink. Directed by Andrew Robinson.

"The Cloud." Teleplay by Tom Szollosi and Michael Piller. Story by Brannon Braga. Directed by David Livingston.

"Coda." Written by Jeri Taylor. Directed by Nancy Malone.

"Course: Oblivion." Teleplay by Bryan Fuller & Nick Sagan. Story by Bryan Fuller. Directed by Anson Williams.

"Day of Honor." Written by Jeri Taylor. Directed by Jesus Salvador Treviño.

"Deadlock." Written by Brannon Braga. Directed by David Livingston.

"Death Wish." Teleplay by Michael Piller. Story by Shawn Piller. Directed by James L. Conway.

"Dreadnought." Written by Gary Holland. Directed by LeVar Burton.

*"Elogium."* Teleplay by Kenneth Biller and Jeri Taylor. Story by Jimmy Diggs & Steve J. Kay. Directed by Winrich Kolbe.

"Emanations." Written by Brannon Braga. Directed by David Livingston.

"Faces." Teleplay by Kenneth Biller. Story by Jonathan Glassner and Kenneth Biller. Directed by Winrich Kolbe.

"False Profits." Teleplay by Joe Menosky. Story by George A. Brozak. Directed by Cliff Bole.

"Flashback." Written by Brannon Braga. Directed by David Livingston.

"Innocence." Teleplay by Lisa Klink. Story by Anthony Williams. Directed by James L. Conway.

"Jetrel." Teleplay by Jack Klein & Karen Klein and Kenneth Biller. Story by

James Thornton & Scott Nimerfro. Directed by Kim Friedman.

"Macrocosm." Written by Brannon Braga. Directed by Alexander Singer.

"Meld." Teleplay by Michael Piller. Story by Michael Sussman. Directed by Cliff Bole.

"Phage." Teleplay by Skye Dent and Brannon Braga. Story by Timothy DeHaas. Directed by Winrich Kolbe.

"Prototype." Written by Nicholas Corea. Directed by Jonathan Frakes.

"Resolutions." Written by Jeri Taylor. Directed by Alexander Singer.

"Sacred Ground." Teleplay by Lisa Klink. Story by Geo Cameron. Directed by Robert Duncan McNeill.

## Websites

United Stated Naval Academy website:

usna.edu

United States Air Force Academy website:

usafa.af.mil

Department of the Navy's United States Naval History website:

www.history.navy.mmil/index.html